"I wanted to you're a beaut

As confessions wer better. "And what next?"

"If you think about it…" He spoke tentatively. "My son's suggestion makes perfect sense."

She stared at him, not bothering to hide her shock. "How?"

"We're practically a family now. You look after the kids after school, help them with their homework. We eat dinner together every night. That's more than a lot of households do, or so I hear. I'd love to have a daughter like yours, and my son thinks the world of you."

"I think he's a special kid too, but marriage?" The suggestion was so unexpected she could hardly take it in.

"It would be a good decision for all of us," he told her. "Your daughter gets the father she wants, and neither of us will have to suffer the burden of single parenting. We'll be a team."

His offer sounded good. Too good, in fact, and that scared her. But she wanted a hot and heavy love affair. She'd clung to her dream for so long that she simply couldn't compromise or discard it so easily.

Jessica Matthews's interest in medicine began at a young age, and she nourished it with medical stories and hospital-based television programmes. After a stint as a teenage candy-striper, she pursued a career as a clinical laboratory scientist. When not writing or on duty she fills her day with countless family and school-related activities. Jessica lives in the central United States with her husband, daughter and son.

A MOTHER'S SPECIAL CARE

BY
JESSICA MATTHEWS

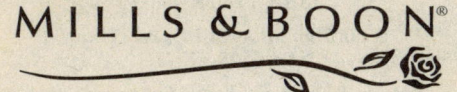

My thanks to David Dugan, MD, whose anesthesiology expertise was invaluable while I wrote this book. Any errors are my own.

To my friends at WARA, especially Theresa Mobley. Our meetings wouldn't be the same without your goodies and marvelous anecdotes.

DID YOU PURCHASE THIS BOOK WITHOUT A COVER?
If you did, you should be aware it is **stolen property** as it was reported *unsold and destroyed* by a retailer. Neither the author nor the publisher has received any payment for this book.

All the characters in this book have no existence outside the imagination of the author, and have no relation whatsoever to anyone bearing the same name or names. They are not even distantly inspired by any individual known or unknown to the author, and all the incidents are pure invention.

All Rights Reserved including the right of reproduction in whole or in part in any form. This edition is published by arrangement with Harlequin Enterprises II B.V. The text of this publication or any part thereof may not be reproduced or transmitted in any form or by any means, electronic or mechanical, including photocopying, recording, storage in an information retrieval system, or otherwise, without the written permission of the publisher.

This book is sold subject to the condition that it shall not, by way of trade or otherwise, be lent, resold, hired out or otherwise circulated without the prior consent of the publisher in any form of binding or cover other than that in which it is published and without a similar condition including this condition being imposed on the subsequent purchaser.

MILLS & BOON and MILLS & BOON with the Rose Device are registered trademarks of the publisher.

*First published in Great Britain 2003
Harlequin Mills & Boon Limited,
Eton House, 18-24 Paradise Road, Richmond, Surrey TW9 1SR*

© Jessica Matthews 2003

ISBN 0 263 83443 3

*Set in Times Roman 10½ on 11½ pt.
03-0503-52702*

*Printed and bound in Spain
by Litografía Rosés, S.A., Barcelona*

CHAPTER ONE

WOULDN'T *anything* go right?

Lori Ames checked the flow rate on her patient's IV infusion pump and was satisfied to see that this particular unit was working properly. How fate had conspired to land her with two faulty pumps in the space of an hour, she didn't know, but it seemed par for the day's course.

As a nurse in St Anne's Post-Anesthesia Care Unit—or the recovery room as most people called it—she was used to expecting the unexpected, but this was ridiculous. Between several emergency additions to the surgery schedule, one of her colleagues calling in sick and several equipment failures requiring the skills of a biomedical technician, her cup of problems was running over.

And that had been *before* she added her failure to find a temporary father for her daughter.

She immediately shelved her personal problems for a later moment. The forty-year-old man who'd arrived in the PACU some thirty minutes ago needed her attention.

Actually, he needed more than her attention. He needed a painkiller which, according to his chart, he shouldn't be needing at all.

Lori placed a PACU lollipop—a mint-flavored sponge of water on a stick—to Allen Clark's mouth and held it for him as he sucked greedily. "It's too soon for you to receive any morphine," she told him in a low, soothing tone. "But I'll let someone know you're hurting."

Allen closed his eyes as he nodded, but not before she'd seen the suffering in his dark eyes.

She strode to the nearest phone and punched in the code for Brad Westmann's pager. He was the nurse-anesthetist responsible for Allen's pain management and the same individual who'd administered his last dose, so Lori wanted to talk to him before she did anything. If he couldn't solve the mystery, then she'd gladly go over his head to Rob Naylor, the orthopedic surgeon who'd repaired her patient's torn rotator cuff, or better yet, Brad's boss, Dr MacKinley Grant.

Her mental picture of the tall, muscularly built Dr Grant had barely formed before he strode into the recovery room. As the chief of anesthesiology, he was ultimately responsible for the care of everyone who was touched by his service, and he took those responsibilities seriously to the point where she wondered if he ever went home. In spite of his near constant presence in the hospital, he didn't micro-manage as some might have, and at times it was reassuring to have him nearby.

However, as Mr Clark moaned, this wasn't one of those times. He had an uncanny ability to spot the most minor of problems at twenty paces and even if her patient hadn't uttered a sound, this case wouldn't have escaped his eagle-eyed notice.

He stopped at the foot of Allen's bed, his gaze riveted to the last blood pressure and oxygen saturation readings displayed. Without a word, he lifted the chart out of its slot on the bed's frame and began reading.

She braced herself for his inevitable questions.

"Who's taking care of this man?" he demanded in a low voice, his eyebrow quirked in his characteristic questioning manner.

She stepped forward. "I am." The staff ratio in the PACU was usually one to one, but occasionally, like now, she had two patients to oversee at once. Her friend, Talia Simmons, was busy with a teenager in the next bed who'd undergone four impacted wisdom teeth extractions, so she would take on the next patient to arrive.

"Are you aware he's in pain?"

His quiet tone didn't fool her. No one spoke loudly in this unit because patients fighting through the fog of anesthesia to wakefulness could misunderstand the comments they heard. Consequently, PACU staff learned to convey their emotion without volume. Right now, the furrow on his forehead and his piercing blue-gray stare spelled trouble.

"Yes, I am."

He tapped the chart. "You haven't given him any relief."

"No—" she began, but before she could defend herself, he tapped the clipboard.

"Why not?"

She straightened her spine at his raised eyebrow, refusing to be intimidated because she'd taken the only course available to her. "He received a dose before he arrived here. About thirty minutes ago."

The fire in his eyes didn't lessen as he frowned at her, but to her relief he readdressed the chart, presumably to verify her claim.

She wanted to explain her doubts about Brad administering the dose in question but Dr Grant's stern expression cautioned her to say as little as possible. Although this wouldn't be the first time Brad's actions hadn't matched his documentation, she couldn't accuse the nurse-anesthetist without proof. So she held her tongue and stole a surreptitious glance at the man beside her.

Dr Grant's light brown hair was short, and as usual, appeared on the unruly side. She'd never quite decided if his windblown appearance was due to a natural wave or his tendency to rake those strands with his fingers whenever he was deep in thought, like he was at the moment.

He was tall, close to her six-foot brother-in-law's height, but he was definitely more solid and more muscular than Tim. Of course, she'd never seen Dr Grant in anything but a scrub suit, but the lightweight cotton couldn't disguise rippling biceps and sinewy quads.

She rarely saw him with a five-o'clock shadow and certainly not at two in the afternoon, but his night on call and their busy morning were most likely responsible. The beginnings of a dark gray tinge filled the slight but sexy dimple in his chin and emphasized the contours of his upper lip.

His maroon scrub suit was rumpled, clearly as a result of the long hours he'd spent in surgery and Recovery while the rest of the world slept peacefully. The town of Redwood, in the heart of the Midwest, was large by small-town standards with its population of fifteen thousand, but the hospital hadn't yet reached the point where the CEO could justify staffing two OR shifts. Everyone from the two anesthesiologists down to the operating room technicians rotated through the on-call schedule in order to handle those cases that couldn't wait until morning. Long days and longer nights weren't uncommon.

Silently begging the phone to ring, Lori released a frustrated sigh, then inhaled a clean, woodsy fragrance. Dr Grant may have worked for nearly twenty hours, but he'd obviously found time for a shower.

"So what were you planning to do?" he asked. "Let him suffer for several more hours?"

"No, I'm waiting for Brad to answer my page." Brad would have to give her a new med order or admit that he hadn't followed through on his own record-keeping. She'd seen the disastrous consequences when nurses had gone out on a limb for him before, and she wasn't about to get caught in the same position if at all possible. Brad didn't mind letting someone else take the blame for his mistakes.

On the other hand, she didn't want to accuse him of a charting error without proof. If she was wrong, she'd be the one appearing troublesome, not him.

Her explanation seemed to appease him, at least for the moment. "Don't wait too long," he advised.

"I won't." She was so sure of Brad's haphazard charting that she was tempted to administer the painkiller, but the threat of causing an overdose held her back. Of the two possible scenarios, it was far better for Mr Allen to suffer for a few more minutes than to recover from the complications of a medication error.

"Where is he?" Dr Grant asked.

"I don't know." That in itself was another strike against Brad in her mental ledger. With his propensity for disappearing without a trace, he should have become a magician rather than a nurse-anesthetist.

The whir of the automatic blood pressure monitor on Mr Leiker, the patient in the next bed, caught her attention. Because this fellow's TURP procedure, or transurethral resection of his prostate hadn't gone well and he'd required multiple units of blood, she kept a close eye on him.

Good thing, too. According to the numbers on the monitor, his blood pressure was dropping. To make matters worse, the heart-rate pattern on the screen changed to one of sinus tachycardia.

The man was losing ground before her eyes.

She rushed to his side and repeated the blood pressure measurement. The numbers were still low, much too low. Not a good sign.

"Does he have a history of heart problems?" Dr Grant asked as he moved to the opposite of the patient's bed to study the monitors.

"No." Lori checked Mr Leiker's bandage and drainage tube. The pads were soaked and the tube was filled with blood. "He shouldn't be bleeding this much." She'd seen cardiac dysrhythmias manifest themselves in her unit before and for a variety of reasons. The cause that came to mind was the same one that Dr Grant voiced a second later.

"Hypovolemia." He'd apparently seen the same signs of

blood loss that she had. With a low volume of blood, the patient was receiving inadequate oxygen throughout his tissues. "Is he cross-matched?"

"He received three units during surgery. When this is empty..." she pointed to the bag hanging on his IV stand "...he won't have any left."

"Call the blood bank and order four more units," Dr Grant ordered. "Get a stat CBC and coagulation studies, too. He may have a clotting problem."

Lori nodded. How ironic to be grateful for Dr Grant's presence when up until a few minutes ago she'd felt the opposite. While she knew what to do, it was nice having a physician nearby to handle whatever might happen. If Mr Leiker's condition deteriorated without further warning or if he went into cardiac arrest, the presence of a physician could make all the difference.

"Who's the surgeon?" he asked.

"Harrington."

"Call him," Dr Grant ordered. "He may have some repair work to do."

Lori moved to Leiker's feet. "I need to—"

He brushed her aside. "I'll take care of it. Make those phone calls."

She didn't argue. While she called the lab and paged Dr Harrington using the special code signifying emergencies in the PACU, Dr Grant elevated Leiker's legs and administered what she assumed was epinephrine. The drug would constrict the blood vessels until they were able to correct the low blood volume.

For the next few minutes the area bustled with activity as the lab personnel arrived and left with their precious blood sample. Dr Harrington arrived on the run and, after conferring with Dr Grant, made arrangements to return to surgery.

The phone rang. Standing the closest to it and expecting to hear from the lab, Lori snatched the handset.

"Hey, Lori. Talia said you're looking for me. What's up?"

Brad spoke her name in a lazy bedroom drawl which irritated her no end. In his late forties, the balding CRNA thought himself a ladies' man but he was more annoying than charming. At least he'd stopped calling the female staff pet names like "lambkins" and "sweet cakes". After several of the more outspoken nurses had threatened a sexual harassment lawsuit, he'd modified his vocabulary.

Lori gritted her teeth and let his syrupy tone slide by without comment. "Mr Clark, the fellow with the rotator cuff repair desperately needs pain meds, but I can't give him any because according to the chart—"

"Oh, yeah, I forgot to tell you—"

Conscious of Dr Grant standing within earshot, she repeated Brad's words. "Forgot to tell me what?"

"I didn't give him his dose."

"Why not? You took time to chart it."

"It's not my fault the vial was empty when I went to draw up the dose," he defended himself. "I got sidetracked before I could hunt down another one."

"It would have been nice to know that when you brought him in here," she said. "I wouldn't be worrying about this man and he wouldn't be lying here, suffering."

"If you recall, I was being paged and didn't have time to chat," he said nastily. "Life in the OR isn't exactly moving along at a snail's pace, you know."

All the more reason for your charting to be accurate, she wanted to say. Clearly Brad thought that working in the PACU was simply a ho-hum routine of taking vitals and mopping up vomit. Little did *he* know of the stresses inherent to this unit or else he was too egoistical to think that someone else might work as hard as he did.

Lori bit back her comment. Arguing with Brad would have to wait for a calmer moment when she didn't have a critically ill patient on her hands. "I have to go. Mr Clark needs his meds now." Fighting the urge to slam the receiver down, she forced herself to replace it with a quiet click.

Idiot, she thought.

Apparently she'd spoken aloud because Dr Grant's voice came from behind her. "I presume that was Brad?"

Her face warmed at least ten degrees. Calling a member of his personal staff an unflattering name wasn't a smart way to win herself over to his good side.

"Yes, it was." Immediately, she hurried to Mr Clark's side, filled a syringe with the required amount of morphine and injected it into his IV port, conscious of Dr Grant's gaze following her every move from the time she began until she disposed of the syringe.

"You'll feel better in a few minutes," she told her pain-ridden patient.

Mr Clark managed a weak chuckle. "Promise?"

She smiled down at him. "You bet. Would you like your lollipop now?"

"Yes."

Once again she moistened his lips and allowed him to suck the fluid from the sponge until he declared he'd had enough.

One problem down, one to go.

By the time the scrub nurses appeared to wheel Mr Leiker back to the OR, the lab had telephoned with his test results and a hard copy report had arrived via their laser printer.

"His hematocrit is low," Dr Grant said as he scanned the printed form before handing it to the OR staff to carry to Dr Harrington. "Coag studies are normal, which is good."

"What do you think happened?" Lori asked Dr Grant, aware of how well they'd functioned together in this emergency—like the proverbial well-oiled machine.

"Either Harrington missed tying a vessel or he nicked

one and didn't realize it,'' he answered. "That guy was just lucky to have such a conscientious nurse looking after him."

Lori's face warmed. She wasn't used to being praised for doing her job, but to have someone of Dr Grant's stature notice...well, that was enough to make anyone glow. It had nothing to do with the fact that this sinfully attractive man was studying her as if he were seeing her for the first time, or so she told herself. "Thanks."

"What was the situation with Brad?"

She might have known that he'd ask. "He didn't administer the dose as charted."

He frowned. "Why not?"

"According to him, he got sidetracked before he could hunt down a new vial."

His expression didn't change. If he wondered, as she had, why Brad hadn't stocked his supplies before the surgery started, he didn't comment.

"It's a good thing you checked on the situation so promptly," he commented. "You saved that man a lot of unnecessary pain."

Two compliments in a row. This was certainly a day for surprises. "Thanks. I try to stay on top of things, especially when—" She stopped herself, unsure how to continue.

"Especially when what?" he prompted.

"It's happened before," she admitted.

"I see." Dr Grant paused, appearing curious. "With all of the nurse-anesthetists, or one in particular?"

She squared her shoulders. "I can't speak for the other PACU nurses, but my experience has only been with one of them."

He ran one hand through his hair, looking as if he intended to say something else, but the moment passed as Dr Rob Naylor, Allen Clark's orthopedic surgeon and a personal friend of hers, walked in and greeted them.

"I just came to check on my patient," Rob said jovially. "How's he doing?"

"Fine." The lines of tension on Mr Clark's face had eased and he was resting comfortably.

"Good," Rob said. "I'll send him to a regular room and you can have another free bed."

Suddenly, the pager on Dr Grant's waistband bleeped and he silenced the noise as he read the number on the display.

"Excuse me," he said politely. "I have to make a phone call." Without waiting for her reply, he headed for the telephone on the nurses' desk across the room.

Lori sensed that Dr Grant would have a talk with Brad but only time would tell if Brad would straighten up his act. In hindsight, Dr Grant's presence had been fortuitous. He'd seen Brad's incompetence for himself and had helped save Leiker's life. Not a bad way to spend the morning.

While he'd always treated her with polite respect—she'd always assumed it was because she was one of the few single women who didn't throw themselves at him—today something had changed. Maybe it was because for the past hour they'd been partners, drawn together by the common goal of keeping Leiker alive. It was hard to remain aloof from someone under those circumstances.

Lori wasn't sure if she liked this new development. She'd caught herself on more than one previous occasion wanting to trace the defined lines of his mouth and his sexy chin, to feel his large but infinitely gentle hands splayed across her back. He exuded strength and power and kindness and he possessed something in his gaze that always managed to send awareness humming through her entire body.

How could she keep her thoughts and hormones under strict control if he cast his rare but extremely special smile in her direction on a regular basis?

At times, Lori had wanted to erase the anguish in his

eyes, but she refused to get lumped in the same category as so many other women who wanted to snag a successful, handsome widower. She worked with him on a daily basis and didn't want personal issues to interfere with their colleague-of-sorts relationship. Her job was too important to jeopardize.

No matter how things had changed this afternoon, she couldn't completely let down her guard. After falling for one needy soul, she'd wound up pregnant and married at eighteen. She'd struggled for the last eight years, two of them with Glenn, and she'd lost her desire to repeat the experience. Someone else would have to exorcize Dr Grant's ghosts.

If she decided to invite another man into her life, it would be one who, as her sister described, had his head screwed on straight and who was the proverbial open book.

Rob broke into her thoughts, making her realize that Talia had joined them and both were staring at her strangely. "Why the frown?" he asked.

"I was about to ask the same thing," Talia said.

"No reason." Lori flashed them a smile. "Just woolgathering. It's been my first opportunity all day."

"I've been thinking, too," Rob said. "About what you asked me earlier. About Ronnie needing a dad."

Talia's green eyes popped open. "Gosh, Lori. When did you decide to remarry?" As a twenty-four-year-old newlywed, she'd been unsuccessfully trying to organize dates for Lori with her husband's bachelor buddies.

"I haven't," Lori answered her friend as she glared at Rob for mentioning the subject in front of a woman who'd embraced matchmaking as her newest hobby. If she didn't explain, she couldn't begin to imagine what Talia would say or do.

"I just want someone who'll go to school with Veronica and act as her dad for the school's 'Donuts for Dads' breakfast program. A friend, an uncle or a grandfather-type would do just as well." Since Ronnie's only uncle lived eight hours away and she had no grandfather, that left the final category of friend, which was why she'd asked Rob to fill the role.

Unfortunately, he was committed to attending an orthopedic conference on the same day in Chicago. What a shame that technology hadn't progressed to allow people to be in two different places at once.

She addressed Rob hopefully. "Did they change the date of your meeting?"

He shook his head. "Sorry. I wish they would because I'd love to go with Ronnie."

"I know." She'd first met Rob, and his wife and daughter, at St Anne's annual spring picnic shortly after they'd moved to Redwood. Veronica, or Ronnie as she preferred to be called, had caused a stir when she'd broken her wrist by falling off the park's monkey bars. As one of the town's two orthopedic surgeons, Rob had immediately taken charge of Ronnie while Gail had taken Lori under her wing. Eventually, their sixteen-year-old, Susannah, had begun babysitting Ronnie before school in what soon became the perfect arrangement for everyone. Susannah's parents didn't have to drag her out of bed each morning and Lori went to work secure in knowing her daughter was looked after in spite of the early hour.

If Rob could help her, he would.

"What about Doug Halforan?" Talia asked, referring to one of the OR technicians.

Lori shook her head. "Doug's a nice guy, but he turns beet red whenever a woman talks to him. I can't imagine how he'd act in front of a room full of inquisitive children."

"There's always Brad."

"I'm not that desperate. I can just imagine what he'd assume if I asked him to accompany my daughter to school." She shuddered, imagining his feral grin and his sly winks. "No, thank you."

"What about someone from another department?" Rob suggested. "Surely you've met more people in the hospital than those who work in surgery."

"I've met some and know their names, but they're basically strangers. I couldn't possibly ask such a favor."

"You realize that you're a widow, not a nun," Talia reminded her.

Lori sighed. "I know." Perhaps she was ridiculous to hold onto her dreams of a fairy-tale romance, but this time she wouldn't settle for anything less.

Rob pursed his mouth into a thoughtful line. "What about your neighbors?"

"Men are few and far between on my street," Lori said wryly. "The city should change the name from Willow Lane to Widow Lane."

"It's not that bad, is it?" Talia asked.

"We have three men living on the entire block," Lori told her. "One constantly complains about Ronnie riding her bicycle across his driveway, another needs a motorized wheelchair for mobility and the third has just been arrested for possession of marijuana with intent to sell. Who would you choose?"

Talia grimaced. "I see your point."

"Actually," Rob said slowly, "I believe I know someone who would work out nicely."

"Who?"

"Mac." Rob inclined his head in Dr Grant's direction.

Talia's sharply indrawn breath caused her to cough, but Lori ignored her as the idea sent a shiver of something— anxiety or maybe delight—down to her toes. "Dr Grant? Why him?"

"You two would be good together," he insisted.

"Yeah right."

"I'm serious. He's so perfect, I don't know why I didn't

think of him before." Rob appeared as proud as if he'd just unraveled a mystery of the universe.

"Rob, I've never had a conversation with him that didn't revolve around the hospital," Lori protested. "I don't know anything about him."

"You know he has a son in Ronnie's grade at school," Rob said.

"Only because you told me. He's worse than a clam when it comes to talking about himself or his family."

"If you want my vote," Talia interjected with enthusiasm. "I think you should ask him."

"Don't you have a patient to look after?" Lori asked crossly.

Talia giggled. "Yeah, which is why I put my two cents' worth in early." With that, she returned to her monitors.

Rob folded his arms across his chest. "See? Even Talia agrees with me."

Lori glared at him, irritated by the broad smile on his weathered face. "I still don't understand why you think he's so perfect."

"It's simple, really. Have you forgotten that the week after 'Donuts for Dads' is 'Muffins for Moms'?"

"How did you know that?" She'd asked for the day off, but hadn't shared her reasons with anyone.

"Susannah might be a teenager, but I can remember back to when she was eight. I do have a few cells of functioning gray matter up here." He tapped his forehead. "Anyway, you two can help each other out. Mac doesn't have a wife, so his son is in the same boat as Ronnie."

Joining forces with Dr Grant for two simple school functions seemed like an innocent and logical solution to a mutual problem, but was the problem a mutual one?

"Maybe he's already found someone to go with his son," she pointed out. "Maybe Dr Grant has a girlfriend."

"He doesn't."

Lori wasn't really surprised by the news. From the bits

and pieces of conversations she'd overheard from the other physicians and the way his cool stare froze even the most determined flirts, Dr Grant acted as interested in dating as she did. Then again, it could have meant that he was already spoken for and didn't want to publicize the fact.

"Who went with him last year?" she asked.

"Their housekeeper, Martha. As of a week ago, she moved to Iowa to be closer to her grandchildren. Mac's on his own."

"What about an aunt, a grandmother?"

"His sister lives in Portland. Corey doesn't have any grandparents either. And, before you ask, his in-laws won't be of any help. They haven't been in touch for years."

"Why not?" The idea seemed far-fetched. "Surely they'd want to see their grandson."

"You'd think so but, according to Mac, they don't." His tone became pleading. "For Corey's sake, and Ronnie's, please work something out."

She really didn't want to approach Dr Grant for something so personal, but her daughter desperately wanted a father figure to accompany her on this one day. It was too easy to imagine his son hoping for the same minor miracle and being disappointed, all because she was too timid.

"You didn't mention this to him, did you?" she asked, remembering how a short time ago he'd acted as if he'd wanted to say something and hadn't.

Rob appeared affronted. "Of course not. The idea just came to me a few minutes ago. If you want me to lay the groundwork, though, I will."

"That's quite all right. I'll talk to Mac, er, Dr Grant myself." She was already in trouble if she was starting to think of him by the nickname Rob used.

"But if he takes offense," she warned him, "I'm holding you responsible."

"It's a deal. Now that we have that settled, I believe my patient is waiting for me."

So was hers. Yet as she checked Mr Clark's vital signs again she wondered if she could possibly follow through with this idea. Talking to Dr Grant had never been a problem but, then, work-related subjects were safe topics.

She tried to think of a way to weave the upcoming Parent-Teacher Association programs into her next conversation, but her opening lines seemed contrived and silly. He was sure to think she'd lost her good sense, if not her mind.

How did one ask the most taciturn physician on the staff to be a stand-in father?

CHAPTER TWO

"This isn't a good time to page me." Mac spoke on the phone to his eight-year-old son as he settled behind the nurses' desk.

"I can't help it, Dad," Corey protested. "I need your permission to go home with Ronnie today so we can work on our science project. Her mom is taking her to the Parent Resource Center to cut out planets and stuff, and we need to work on this together."

Ronnie and the feminine pronoun didn't go together. "Ronnie's a girl?" Mac asked for clarification.

"Yeah, Dad. I told you about her, remember?"

He wasn't sure that he did, but if Corey said so, he'd take his word for it. Mac rubbed his hand over his face, wishing once again that he didn't feel totally lost without Martha, his combination housekeeper and nanny.

"Anyway," Corey continued over the telephone, "we have to pair up for our project on the solar system, and Ronnie is my partner. So, Dad, can I go with her after school? They have really neat stuff at the resource center."

Mac heard the plea in his son's voice and instantly guilt attacked him. "Why don't I take you tomorrow on my afternoon off?"

"It's closed on Wednesdays, Dad. We have to turn our project in on Friday. Today's the best time to go."

Mac knew that he needed to spend more time with Corey. His sister had preached on the subject for years, but juggling his parenting responsibilities and medical profession without Martha to guide him was like a surgeon operating with his eyes closed. For the past week he'd suffered tremendous feelings of inadequacy and failure, and situations like today's made it appear as if those sentiments wouldn't lessen any time soon.

He offered another suggestion. "What if I try to pick you up by four-thirty? We can go then."

"You'll be late," Corey predicted without rancor. "You always are."

"Not always," he protested.

"Most of the time."

That much was true, which was why Mac simply had to find someone to take Martha's position, and soon. He didn't want to worry about Corey waiting at school like a forgotten child, but he couldn't walk away from the hospital whenever he felt like it either.

"The place closes at five," Corey added. "Even if you weren't late, I wouldn't be able to get everything done."

Mac ran one hand through his hair. Corey was right—thirty minutes wouldn't allow him to make an adequate start—but knowing it only served to spotlight Mac's inadequacies with blinding clarity. In this case, he didn't have any choice but to rely on the kindness of strangers.

"Are you sure Ronnie's mother won't mind?"

"Ronnie says it's OK, but you can ask her mom yourself."

"Is she there at school?"

"No, Dad." Hearing Corey's long-suffering tone, Mac could visualize his bespectacled son rolling his eyes. "She works in the hospital with you."

He tried to think of a woman who had a daughter named Ronnie, but came up blank. It wasn't surprising, though. He didn't spend time visiting with the staff. "She does?"

"Her name is Mrs Ames."

Immediately his eyes were drawn to Lori, who at the moment was performing her quarter-hour checks. "Lori?"

"I'm not sure. Do you know more than one Mrs Ames?"

"No."

"Then it must be her." He sounded very practical for one so young.

"I guess so." This shed new light on the situation. If Corey had told him about Ronnie and her mother, he couldn't believe that he'd forgotten. "Did you tell me about her mother before?"

"Ronnie just told me, so how could I?"

That one detail gave him some consolation.

"Then is it OK?" Corey persisted.

"Sure," he said. "I'll pick you up at her house after five."

"Thanks, Dad. I gotta go."

Before Mac could ask for the address, a dial tone filled his ear. It wasn't any great problem, he thought as he stared across the room. He'd simply ask Lori as soon as she had a free minute.

He waited patiently, watching her gentle movements as she dealt with Mr Clark. He'd always felt comfortable in her presence, more so than with most of her colleagues, although in the interests of self-preservation he'd taken great pains to hide it. The friendly glint in her eye could easily turn into the sly, calculating gaze of so many other women on the prowl, and he'd hate to see that happen. In any event, he was still too much in love with his wife's memory to be entertaining thoughts of another woman, no matter how personable, how charming, how open and honest, and how attractive he found her.

Lori's hair was the color of polished oak, and clearly long enough to fashion into her usual knot at the back of her head. During rare moments of fancy, he wondered what those shiny tresses would look like if she let them hang free, but decided it was better if he didn't know.

Her features were girlish, her cheeks rosy with good health, her fair skin tanned. He rarely saw her without a soft smile for both staff and patients, including days when everyone else's tempers were frayed.

She was taller than average, but the top of her head only came to his chin. He'd noticed, because he could often smell her floral-scented shampoo when he stood next to her. Her body reminded him of the quiet and easy grace of a figure skater as she glided across the recovery room on silent feet.

During her first few days at St Anne's, he'd heard of her widowed and single-parent status, and as time had passed he'd fully expected some lucky man to claim her. She was friendly, caring and seemed like a woman who was tailor-made for a role as wife and mother, so who could resist? Yet when Talia had brought cake to celebrate Lori's twenty-seventh birthday last month, he couldn't understand why she wasn't any closer to adding a ring to her finger.

Whatever her reasons for remaining single, he couldn't deny that Lori Ames was one classy lady.

Something akin to jealousy stirred inside him as he imagined Corey basking in the sunshine of her smile. It had been ages since he'd spent time with a woman who understood his work and was near his own age, and to his surprise he discovered that he missed the experience. Sure, he visited with Rob's wife Gail, but seeing his friends together in comfortably wedded bliss only emphasized how alone he really was.

His self-imposed penance.

Blythe Monroe, one of his nurse-anesthetists, blonde and thirty-eight, came in and spoke in hushed tones to Talia. A quick swipe of her pen and one more patient was allowed to leave the recovery room. As Talia readied the youth for discharge, he realized that if he didn't approach Lori now, before he was scheduled to administer the first of several epidurals in his pain clinic, he'd lose his opportunity.

Unwilling to waste another moment, Mac strode in her direction and stood at the foot of Mr Clark's bed. She glanced at him and he saw the question in her chocolate brown eyes.

"Where do you live?" he asked without preamble.

"Wh-what?"

He rephrased his comment. "What's your address? My son just called and asked for permission to go with you to the Resource Center."

Understanding replaced her puzzlement. "I didn't realize Corey was your son."

Her mention of Corey by name made it seem as if he was the last one to be included in his son's plans. The idea rankled. "You knew about this excursion?"

"Oh, yes. Last night Ronnie asked if we could go after school. She'd explained how they were working in groups and I volunteered to take Corey if he wanted to join us. Although I didn't know until you brought it up that you'd given your permission."

"Oh." He felt marginally better. "Then you don't mind if he tags along?"

She smiled. "Not at all. Shall I drop him off at home after we're done?"

"I'd rather pick him up at your house. In case I'm late."

"No problem. Our address is 5235 Wid—er, Willow Lane."

He wondered why her face had turned an endearing shade of pink. Was she uncomfortable with giving out such personal information? Or was she simply uncomfortable with sharing it with him?

"Do you know where it is?" she asked.

He nodded. "Then I'll see you later."

It didn't make sense why his afternoon suddenly seemed brighter, or why he found himself eager to complete his scheduled appointments. Corey had gone home with other friends before and Mac hadn't felt like he stood on the brink of a new discovery.

It was pure curiosity, he decided as he scrubbed, gowned and gloved. He'd seen Lori Ames at work and now he wanted to see her in her home environment. Of course, he'd only have a glimpse, but it would be enough.

He strode into the surgery suite and greeted his patient, who was already on the table.

"Hello, Mrs Eyestone. I presume your pain hasn't gone away on its own, has it?"

"I wish," the sixty-year-old woman said. She'd been in a car accident six months ago that had left her with a herniated disk, a pinched nerve and chronic back pain. Her family physician had run a battery of tests to rule out other etiologies before he had referred her to Mac. In fact, Brad had been in the same car accident, but his injuries had been minor.

"Does it still hurt in the same area?" he asked.

She nodded her graying head. "Lower back and down into my left leg."

"Muscles still weak?" He referred to her quadriceps.

"Oh, yes."

The MRI, or magnetic resonance imagery, had revealed a herniation in the L3-4 disks, which fit the signs and symptoms Mrs Eyestone displayed. Because of the rupture, she suffered a nerve root inflammation, which Mac hoped to alleviate.

"OK. Let's see if I can't do something to give you some relief." Mac nodded to the nurse, who rolled her into a side position.

"You'll feel a pinprick," he warned before he injected the lidocaine into her spinal column, between the third and fourth lumbar disks, to anesthetize the area. "How does it feel?"

"Much better," she answered.

Her comment confirmed that the tip of the needle was in the epidural space at the appropriate level. After swapping syringes, he injected the corticosteroid that would reduce the inflammation.

A few minutes later, he was done.

"Your symptoms should improve," he told her as he rose. "If they aren't completely gone in one to two weeks, we'll bring you back. I want you to call my office next week and let us know how you're doing so we can decide if we should schedule you for a repeat visit."

"All right. Thank you, Doctor."

Mac moved on through his list of tasks, which weren't many since today was a light surgery day. He was fortunate that in Redwood nurse-anesthetists were allowed to function more independently than their counterparts in larger cities. There, they worked under the direct supervision of an anesthesiologist who was responsible for the induction itself.

During his days in the teaching hospital, he could oversee up to four of his subordinates at a time. Here, he was still technically responsible for them, but when he or his colleague, Josh Barnett, weren't on duty, the surgeon took over the supervisory role. Otherwise Mac would work longer hours than he did now.

The hours ticked past. He knew without peeking in the PACU that Lori had left for the day. For the first time in as long as he could remember, he found it difficult to concentrate on the job at hand. Five o'clock wouldn't come soon enough.

"Mom, we're hungry."

"I know, dear. Dinner is ready right now. You and Corey can wash up while I bring the food to the table." Lori removed the hamburger patties from her inexpensive barbecue grill and replaced the lid. She'd love to own one that used gas rather than briquets and starter fluid, but after she'd sold their home to pay her husband's debts after his accident, such things had become a luxury.

"Can we eat outside?"

"Do you want to?" she asked the two children.

Corey's eyes brightened, but he looked at Ronnie before he nodded.

"We do," Ronnie affirmed.

"There are a lot of bugs," she warned. It had been an Indian summer day and the insect population had come out of their hidey-holes for one last fling before the cold snap hit.

"We don't mind," Corey said.

"Let's compromise," Lori said. "We'll fill our plates indoors, then sit outside to eat."

"OK," the two chorused.

Corey started to follow Ronnie inside, presumably in search of a sink, soap and a towel, but he stopped at the door. "If my dad comes, can I still stay and eat with you?" He pushed his black, oval-shaped, wire-rimmed glasses up his nose.

Lori smiled. "Of course."

A broad smile appeared on his face before he hurried after Ronnie.

She couldn't help but compare the two third-graders. Her daughter was a bright, vivacious child who was constantly in motion, and her personality shone as brightly as her copper-colored hair. Corey, by contrast, appeared much more quiet, studious and somber than other children his age which made their willingness to be together so unusual.

He'd seemed unsure of himself around Lori at first, but as she'd talked to him about his vision for their project and had helped him find his supplies, he'd relaxed. By the end of their session at the resource center, she'd been flattered by his insistence on hearing her opinion. It was as if he wanted her approval and her heart went out to the motherless boy. Why Dr Grant didn't talk about his son or display each new school photograph he carried in his wallet like every other proud parent, she didn't know.

And thinking of the anesthesiologist, she would never have believed that Corey was his offspring. Corey's hair, while appearing as if a trim was past due, was as black as midnight and as straight as a board, while his father's was light brown with a natural wave. Their skin tones were different also, with Corey's having a more olive hue than his father's. Mac's features seemed to be a blend of various cultures whereas Corey's showed distinct signs of Spanish ancestry. Obviously the youngster looked like his mother since the only evident traits of Mac were the dimple in his chin and the shape of his mouth.

Corey wasn't tall for his age but, then, boys didn't sprout until they were older. She wondered what he'd look like when he was sixteen, or twenty. He'd probably have to fight the girls off, unless he developed his father's cold stare.

Lori balanced the plate of burgers and her utensils as she walked into the kitchen. Minutes later, she was back outside, seated at the picnic table with her two charges, their full plates and glasses of milk at hand.

"This is really good." Ketchup smudged Corey's cheek, but Lori simply passed out napkins for later use.

"I'm glad you like it," she said.

"We hardly ever have barbecued stuff," he said between bites.

"You don't?" Whenever her brother-in-law Tim was responsible for a meal, he always threw something on the grill. She assumed most men would do the same.

"Oh no. Martha, our housekeeper, did all the cooking. Now that she's gone, we've been going to a lot of restaurants."

"Really." Lori found that interesting.

Corey nodded. "Dad says he isn't good in the kitchen. Maybe you could teach him."

"Maybe," Lori answered. Somehow, she couldn't see herself sharing recipes with Dr Grant, but stranger things had happened. After all, for a man so totally immersed in his profession, he had a home and a son, so he did have a life outside St Anne's walls.

"How long has your housekeeper been gone?" Ronnie asked.

"It's been a week," Corey answered. "I really miss her."

The sadness in his voice brought a lump to Lori's throat and she struggled to swallow. "I'm sure she misses you, too," she said gently.

"She lived with us the longest."

Ronnie's mouth formed a perfect O. "You've always had a housekeeper?"

"Just since I was two."

"Wow, Mom," Ronnie exclaimed. "Too bad we can't have a housekeeper. Wouldn't it be nice not to have any chores?"

"It would," Lori agreed, "but it's not going to happen, so don't waste your time dreaming about it."

Ronnie spoke to Corey. "Is that when your mom died? When you were two?"

"Nah," he said. "She died when I was born. I lived with my aunt until then."

He spoke very matter-of-factly about a story that tugged at Lori's heartstrings. According to Rob, Mac was thirty-five, which meant that his life had turned upside down at the age of twenty-seven and probably still in medical school. Suddenly, the bleakness in Mac's eyes made sense.

"Dad's trying to find someone to live with us," he added, "but he says that Martha is irr—irr—"

Although he couldn't quite get the word out, Lori guessed at it. "Irreplaceable?"

Corey nodded. "That's it. One lady will clean but not cook, and one will cook but not do laundry. Nobody wants to move in so I won't be alone so much."

Her protective instincts reared up as she imagined a young boy fending for himself in an empty house while

Mac's long hours kept him from home. How could he *think* of allowing such a thing!

"You're totally by yourself?" she asked. Although it seemed rather underhanded to coax private information out of his son, her concern over Corey took precedence. Mac surely knew the dangers of leaving a child by himself. He couldn't be that irresponsible, could he?

"Only after school," Corey hastened to say. "Which is why Dad's so anxious to hire someone to live with us."

It made her feel marginally better to know that Corey's plight was only temporary. Yet she knew how easily "temporary" could become "permanent".

"What do you do when your dad is on call?" Lori counted her blessings for Susannah and how she met Ronnie's babysitting needs so well. She couldn't imagine what she'd do if her job was as busy and as unpredictable as a physician's.

"For now, our neighbor comes over, but Dad doesn't want to im—im—"

"Impose?"

Once again, Corey nodded. This time, he raked one hand through his hair in a motion characteristic of his father's. "Since Martha left, he's been trying to stay at home more. Last night was the first time he was gone for a long time. Mrs Boyd, from next door, stayed with me all night."

"I'm done," Ronnie pronounced.

Corey shoved the last bite in his mouth and chewed. "Me, too," he said, clearly ready to participate in whatever activity Ronnie suggested.

"Did you finish your homework?" Lori asked.

"No," they chorused. "But we don't have much."

"Then you'll be able to finish it lickety-split. I'm sure Dr Grant will appreciate having time to do something fun with Corey before bedtime."

"It won't matter," Corey volunteered. "Dad usually

works in his study and I play computer games or get on the internet and chat with my cousins."

"Oh?" Once again, she wondered at Mac's relationship with his son. She couldn't imagine not spending at least an hour playing board games or cards with her daughter, taking the time to discuss their day or just giggle and have girl-talk.

"We can do it later. Mrs Cooper didn't assign us much since we're supposed to be working on our science projects," Ronnie told her.

"Now," Lori commanded. Then, softening her tone, she added, "Afterwards, we'll play Go Fish or Old Maid. And don't forget to take your plates with you."

"OK."

By the time Lori had cleaned up the kitchen, it was after six-thirty and Mac still hadn't arrived. Although she could imagine any number of possible explanations for the delay, she was concerned on Corey's behalf. What if she hadn't taken him with her today? Would he have been at home by himself, eating whatever he could find in the refrigerator, or would he simply have gone without?

Not likely, she decided. With all the pizza deliveries available, Corey certainly wouldn't starve, but the idea of an eight-year-old at home alone for hours on end bothered her nonetheless.

It's not your concern, she told herself. Mac's a responsible parent. He would have made other arrangements if she hadn't brought Corey with them.

All things considered, she understood why young Corey had wanted her approval so much. Clearly, Martha had been a major influence in his life and now the poor boy was practically lost without her. Mac might be trying to adjust his schedule, but Corey would probably be left on his own far more than he should be at his age.

The question uppermost in her mind now was should she ask Mac to be Ronnie's stand-in dad? If he could hardly find time for his own son, he certainly couldn't carve out additional minutes of his day for her daughter. Rob might think Mac was perfect for the job, but sometimes the logical choice wasn't the best. Fortunately, Ronnie was too caught up with her guest and her school project to mention the father-daughter breakfast, but once Corey went home the subject was bound to surface.

What should she do?

Determined to forget all else but entertaining the two, Lori suggested a rousing card game. By seven, she'd been officially crowned "Old Maid" twice, to both Ronnie's and Corey's delight, and it appeared she could earn the designation for a third time when the doorbell rang.

She glanced at Corey to test his reaction and was surprised to find disappointment rather than excitement. She unfolded her legs in order to rise from her spot on the floor next to the children.

"You can leave your cards," Ronnie said a trifle too innocently.

Corey smiled with a toothless grin. "We won't peek."

"That's right—you won't," she said, holding her last three cards to her chest in a theatrical pose. "I'm taking them with me."

Amid their giggles, Lori answered the door. "Hi," she said, suddenly aware that her rapid heart rate wasn't due to the fun she'd been having. Seeing Mac on her porch, looking tired but still inordinately handsome in a gray dress shirt and black trousers, made her realize how unkempt she must look in her blue leggings and oversized white T-shirt.

"Sorry I'm late," he said. "I had a few last-minute referrals to my pain clinic and then—"

"You don't need to explain," she said. "Won't you come in?"

As he crossed the threshold to stand in her living room, his shoulders seemed more broad than she remembered, and the space in her house became smaller than usual. It was a silly wish, but she hoped he wouldn't see the threadbare carpet or notice her cheap furniture. Strangely enough, she wanted to impress him, not gain his pity.

"Dr Grant, this is my daughter, Veronica."

"It's nice to meet you, Ronnie," Mac said politely.

He'd surprised Lori by using Ronnie's nickname without being told. Somehow, it added another point in his favor.

Corey rose, but didn't run to embrace his father as Lori had seen other children do. "Hi, Dad."

"Hello, yourself. Did you have a good time today?" Mac asked.

"Yeah, I did. We just have to arrange our pictures and the fact bubbles on the posterboard and we're done."

"That's nice," Mac said, sounding formally polite, which struck Lori as odd. Was Mac uncomfortable, being around his own son?

"I thought we'd stop for a burger on the way home," he added.

"We've already eaten," Ronnie interrupted. "Mom made extra for you, if you want."

"Thank you, but—" he began.

"The hamburgers were really good," Corey added. "You can eat while we finish our game."

Indecision appeared on Mac's face but the plea in Corey's eyes made her decision for her. If Mac accepted the invitation, she'd have a few more minutes to bolster her courage before she asked for her favor.

"Please stay," she encouraged. "As Ronnie said, we have plenty. It will only take a minute to get everything ready."

He raked his hand through his hair. "Don't go to any trouble just for me."

"It's no trouble at all." She headed for the kitchen, but not before she brandished her cards at the children. "I'm still taking these for safekeeping."

"Mom," Ronnie wailed.

"We'll play at the table while Dr Grant eats. In the meantime, why don't you two show off your project?"

"OK." The two immediately began emptying their folders of artwork while Lori reheated a meat patty and filled Mac's plate with several dollops of potato salad and a handful of carrot sticks. She placed a bowl of grapes in the center of the table for dessert.

Mac joined her five minutes later. "It's nothing fancy," she said as she placed his meal in front of him. A man who could afford a live-in housekeeper probably ate gourmet meals on china instead of simple fare on chipped dinnerware, but she'd chosen her best. His table was probably solid oak or something similar while hers had come from a secondhand store when she'd first gotten married. Fortunately, her apple-patterned tablecloth hid all of the blemishes.

"I'm not choosy. Corey mentioned how the three of you ate outdoors."

Lori grinned. "Only because the weather co-operated." She chose a chair beside his. "OK, kids. Let's get back to our game."

The old maid card slowly made its way from Lori to Ronnie and on to Corey. With each move, the room resounded with groans of dismay and chortles of delight. Lori stole a glance in Mac's direction, and to her surprise found him wearing an amused—and at times amazed—expression as he ate.

Her concentration disappeared. As his lips closed around the tines of his fork, she wondered what his kiss would be like. As his long fingers casually held his carrot sticks, she imagined how his touch would feel. As he smiled, she wanted it directed at her.

Heaven help her if he filled in for Ronnie at school. She'd really have trouble focusing on her job if, when she looked at him, she saw a handsome single man instead of an extremely competent physician.

With her thoughts traveling down this troublesome trail, she absent-mindedly chose a card from Corey's hand. Instantly, Corey guffawed and Lori saw she'd chosen the old maid card. Mac's wide smile, of proportions she hadn't seen before, caught her off guard. *What a truly handsome man.*

Not only had the lines of his face softened, but his eyes sparkled with warmth as well. What a shame that he didn't unbend more often.

"I got you," Corey crowed, as Ronnie laughed aloud and wriggled on her chair.

"Not for long," Lori vowed as she turned to Ronnie. Positioning her remaining two cards, she waited for her daughter to choose.

With the tip of her tongue poking out of the side of her mouth, Ronnie narrowed her eyes as she studied her choices without moving a muscle. Quicker than a blink, she pulled one from Lori's hand and held it on display. "Mom lost—again!"

While Ronnie and Corey gave each other high fives, Lori shook her head. "I'm going to have to find a different game to play with you two."

"Mom lost *three* times," Ronnie announced with the enthusiasm of someone reporting a new record. "She always ends up being the old maid."

Being referred to as an old maid, even though it was all in fun, suddenly made Lori feel ill at ease. Why point out the obvious, especially to an eligible bachelor who'd have women flocking over him if he'd send out the slightest of encouraging signals?

She forced a light note into her voice. "I guess I'm not very lucky." Then, before he could read her double meaning, she handed her cards to Ronnie. If she was going to ask the all-important question, she'd rather do so without an audience.

"Would you two, please, put your toys away while I talk to Dr Grant?"

The two rushed off to obey. Mac leaned back in his chair, his plate now empty. "I don't mind if you call me Mac," he said offhandedly. "I've always called you by your first name."

"Sure. OK." She felt as awkward as a teenage wallflower standing next to the captain of the football team at a school dance.

"Thanks for the meal."

"You're welcome. As I said, it was nothing fancy."

"The simple things in life are usually the best."

Hearing Corey's and Ronnie's laughter coming from the other room, she agreed.

A slight frown tugged at the corners of his mouth. "I've never seen him as animated as he is now."

"It took him a while to warm up, but I think he had a good time. We've enjoyed having him visit." She hesitated. "He told us about your housekeeper and how you're looking for someone to take her place."

"I hope we find someone soon," he confessed. "I don't like Corey being a latch-key child."

His admission encouraged her to stick with her plan, for Ronnie's sake. "I know. I'm lucky to have Rob's daughter, Susannah, to watch Ronnie before school. I'm also fortunate that my shift usually ends so I can pick her up at three-thirty every afternoon." She traced the outlines of several apples on the tablecloth with her fingernail.

"Am I making you nervous?" he asked.

His gaze, though piercing as usual, seemed warmer, his tone amused. Lori didn't see any point in denying the truth. A calm, collected woman wouldn't trace tablecloth designs.

Lori placed her hands on her lap. "It's not you. I mean, we work together all the time and I don't jump out of my skin when you're nearby." She managed a smile. "It's just that it's not easy for me to ask people I don't know very well for a favor."

"I understand, but if it will make you feel better, I'll warn you that I don't bite. At least, not away from the hospital." The corners of his mouth twitched and his voice held a light-hearted quality that she usually didn't hear.

Unbidden, she pictured his lips against her neck, showering her skin with little love bites. Immediately, she forced away the image.

"I know. If it weren't for Ronnie, I wouldn't ask at all," she hastened to add. "I talked to Rob and he can't help me."

Mac raised one eyebrow, as she'd seen many times before, but on this occasion it reflected interest rather than cynicism.

"You see, the school is having a father-daughter breakfast in a few days."

"Ah, yes," he said, nodding. "'Donuts for Dads'."

At least he was attuned to the events at the school, which meant he wasn't totally oblivious to his son's life. "Anyway," she continued, "Ronnie would like to go, but she needs a dad and Rob will be out of town. Would...would you be willing to take her father's place?"

CHAPTER THREE

MAC had come to a point in his life where he believed that nothing would surprise him. Between the horrors of medicine, losing his wife and watching the nightly news, he thought he was immune to the unusual.

Apparently, not so.

Lori's request had caught him offguard for several seconds, but he'd learned to think on his feet when the unexpected occurred. As he considered his own problems with single parenting and her comment about picking up her daughter after school, a potentially workable idea began to form.

"If you can't," she hastened to say, "that's all right. I just thought we could, if you were willing, that is, help each other out. Corey's mother-son breakfast is coming up and if he needed someone to accompany him, I thought it might be a fair trade if I went as your wi—, er, his guest."

"I see," he said, stalling for time as he ran through the aspects of his own plan.

"If I went in your wife's place, or you went in my husband's, it wouldn't mean we had a romantic interest," she hastened to say. "Someone just coined a few catchy jingles. The idea is for kids to learn what different jobs and careers are available to them and for parents to become involved at school." Her laugh sounded forced. "But, then, you went through this last year, so why am I explaining it to you?"

As she rubbed the back of her neck, the curly strands of her hair fell over one shoulder. Mac idly wondered what it would feel like to run his hands through her long, soft tresses.

"If you have someone else in mind," she rambled on, "then forget I said anything. I just had a wild idea and...and...you won't have to do anything at the breakfast except sit with Ronnie, eat donuts and drink coffee."

"And talk about my job," he reminded her.

"You wouldn't need a formal speech or anything. A few words will do."

The nurse who usually appeared calm and collected in any sort of emergency was babbling and Mac found it intensely amusing to see her at such a loss. He understood why she'd been so anxious.

She thought he'd refuse.

For a man who wasn't doing a bang-up job with parenting his own son, he should give her an unequivocal and resounding "no", but he was in a bind as well. Her mention of a fair trade encouraged him to accept.

"If Ronnie is agreeable then, yes, I'll go in her father's place."

"If your schedule won't allow it," she continued as if he hadn't spoken, "I'll understand."

"I'll go."

Lori rubbed a spot on the tablecloth and avoided his gaze. "Ronnie doesn't know that I've asked you, so don't worry about disappointing her if—"

Mac leaned across the table and covered one of her hands with his, becoming instantly aware of silky skin and fine bones. "I said yes."

She blinked in amazement and Mac realized how expressive her dark eyes were. "Yes?" she echoed.

He nodded.

Her shoulders slumped in obvious relief before she stiffened again. "It's Friday morning, at seven a.m.," she warned him.

"I'll be here." He usually didn't go to the hospital until nine.

"What about Corey? You can't leave him at home alone."

Reluctantly, he released her hand and leaned back in his chair. "Rob's daughter comes here every morning, right?" At her nod, he continued. "I'll bring Corey with me and we'll swap children. He can stay with Susannah and she can deliver him to school, provided you don't object."

She flashed the soft smile she used on her patients, stunning him by its effect on his pulse rate. "Oh, no. That would be fine."

Mac forced himself to focus on their arrangement rather than his response to her smile. He'd definitely been alone far too long if a grin of gratitude and an innocent touch created an ache that begged for release. Then again, he added a full measure of blame to her hair hanging past her shoulders in casual disarray.

"As for helping Corey," she continued, "if I'm not off duty on the day of his breakfast, I'll try to swap my early shift for a later one."

"Fair enough. That brings me to *my* favor," he said as he tried to phrase his request so that she couldn't possibly refuse. "I'd like to propose a trade, and I hope you'll think it's fair."

"What did you have in mind?"

The difficulty of the situation he was about to suggest suddenly occurred to him. If Lori agreed to his plan, he'd encounter her on a daily basis, without the barrier of their profession between them. He'd see her as she was now—relaxed, gorgeous and wearing clothes that were far too sexy for a man who'd lived a celibate life for eight years. He must have masochistic tendencies to put himself in a position of constant temptation, but what choice did he have? For his son, he'd manage. Somehow.

It suddenly struck him as odd that he was even tempted to be disloyal to Elsa's memory. He'd encountered plenty of beautiful women since his wife's death, but none had stirred his interest. What was it about Lori that had caught his eye? And why now?

He drew a bracing breath and concentrated on the conversation at hand instead of his unanswered questions. "You pick up Ronnie every day."

"Most of the time, yes."

"Could Corey stay with you after school? I'd collect him between five and six, although there might be times when I'm late."

"Like tonight."

Mac shrugged as he nodded. "Our arrangement would only be temporary, but I'd be willing to pay you. Including the cost of any meals you provide."

"Your idea of a trade is paying me to look after Corey."

"Yes." After seeing her home's well-worn furnishings and the ten-year-old Pontiac in the driveway, he thought the idea of compensation would cement the deal.

Lori visibly bristled and the smile on her face disappeared. "I don't expect payment from my daughter's friends. And I can certainly afford to feed another mouth or two without taking out a bank loan."

Clearly, he'd touched on the sore spot of her finances. She might have her pride, but so did he. "I'm sorry if I offended you because that wasn't my intent. Corey has visited classmates and vice versa, but this isn't the same. I'm asking for Corey to stay here five afternoons a week, not once in a while."

Two pink spots appeared on her cheekbones. "I apologize for reacting so strongly, but if I choose to help you with Corey, I won't accept your money."

"Why not?" he asked.

"Because."

"Because why?"

"Because it would change things between us," she said a trifle crossly. "Especially at the hospital."

He was momentarily taken aback. "How?"

Lori met his gaze. "At St Anne's, we're colleagues of sorts. Professionals. If you pay me for this, then I become your employee."

"If I *don't* pay you, you're giving me something for nothing," he pointed out. Although he had an instant idea of what he'd like to offer her, he didn't think she'd accept an intimate evening for two with no strings attached as a fair exchange.

"I don't want Corey to think that I'm doing this for any reason other than he's a good kid and I'm willing to be his friend."

"I appreciate the gesture but, contrary to what you think, I get something out of this, too. Knowing I can count on someone is worth a great deal to me. There are a lot of people who aren't reliable unless they receive something in return."

"Then you don't know the right people," she retorted.

"Apparently not." Mac hesitated. "I find it just as difficult to ask for favors as you do. The fact remains, I need a place for Corey. Would you be willing to provide that place or should I look for someone else?"

She hesitated and Mac braced himself for rejection. None of the women he'd interviewed so far wanted to assume responsibility for a little boy. He'd hoped that Lori would be different.

Her glance drifted past his shoulder and her eyes seemed to melt as she smiled. Without looking, he assumed she'd seen one or both kids in the background and her maternal instincts had surfaced. Clearly, she had a soft spot for children. Although he didn't care to exploit people's weaknesses, in this case he would because he was desperate.

"I'd be happy to look after Corey," she said simply.

Mac twisted his body to see Corey and Ronnie standing side by side in the doorway. Corey's wide grin and the pure excitement shining in his dark eyes made Mac feel as if he'd finally done something to earn his son's approval.

He turned back to face Lori. "Tomorrow is my afternoon off, so shall we start on Thursday?"

"That's fine with me. I should warn you though. There are times when I'm late, too, and Ronnie has to walk home."

"As long as Corey has a place to go to where he won't be alone, I don't mind."

"Then it's settled. And you won't forget the school breakfast is at seven on Friday?"

"I'll be here at six forty-five. Sharp."

Later, after they'd returned home and Corey was engrossed in a television program, Mac reflected on the wide grin that hadn't left Corey's face. It was unusual to see his son so taken with a woman he'd just met and rather humbling to realize how Corey had appeared more comfortable with a stranger than with his own father. Yet, it was only understandable. From the moment of Corey's birth and Elsa's death, Corey had been a vivid reminder of Mac's loss and he'd distanced himself from the pain by letting his sister, and later Martha, assume responsibility for the boy's emotional needs.

For a long time he'd resented this little bundle of humanity, but eventually his bitterness had faded. Wiping away tears, hugging a tiny body goodnight and accepting slobbery kisses had chipped away at that destructive emotion until it had disappeared. Yet one fact remained. With Martha to rely upon, he'd allowed the demands of his career to gobble up more and more of his attention. He hadn't realized until recently just how much he'd lost in the process.

Maybe Lori could show him how to build a closer relationship with his son. While he didn't see how they'd function without a housekeeper to handle the details of daily living, he'd like to form the same bond with Corey that she'd clearly formed with her daughter.

He smiled, wondering what his sister would think if she

knew what direction his thoughts had taken. While she'd breathe a sigh of relief and tell him it was about time he came to his senses, she'd also assume that he was ready to give up his lonely existence and seek out female companionship.

Mac didn't think he was ready for that step. Lori Ames was the most promising candidate to date, but cultivating a relationship with one more person would require more time than he simply had available. Juggling his job and Corey's needs were all he could handle at this point, and it still wasn't clear if he could do those two things well. As for those instances when he missed being the other half of a couple, he'd have to continue missing it. He simply wasn't ready to fill Elsa's place.

"This is Alice Fisher," Blythe informed Lori on Friday morning as she wheeled the patient into the PACU. "She sailed through her hysterectomy but I don't think she'll agree with me."

Lori smiled down at fifty-two-year-old Alice, who'd managed a slight grin in spite of being groggy. "I'm Lori and I'll be watching you for the next few hours. If you need anything, I'm only a whisper away."

Alice nodded as her eyelids drifted closed. Lori let her rest quietly while she listened to Blythe's low-pitched recitation.

"Abdominal hysterectomy. No apparent reactions to the propofol or morphine. No underlying diseases or allergies. Because she was already anemic, we gave her two units of packed red cells so we'll repeat her H and H in a few hours."

Lori reviewed the PACU record and noted that everything Blythe had mentioned was already documented and her orders for pain relief were already spelled out. This nurse-anesthetist was thorough, which made Lori's job much easier.

"I'll check on you both later," Blythe finished.

"OK. By the way," Lori said as she began to take the first round of vital signs, "have you seen Dr Grant yet this morning?"

"Sorry. If I do, I'll tell him that you're looking for him."

Afraid the other woman would read the personal interest in her eyes, Lori focused her attention on the red display of oxygen saturation numbers. "Don't bother," she said offhandedly. "It's nothing that can't wait. I'm sure he'll pop in before long. I'll talk to him then."

"Suit yourself."

Lori readjusted the blood pressure cuff and began going through her checklist of vital signs. As the cuff automatically inflated amid a whir and Alice's eyes flew open at the unexpected noise, she explained what she was doing. "I'll be finished in a few minutes and then you can rest."

Alice closed her eyes. "I thought I'd sleep until I went back to my room."

Lori smiled. "We want you to wake up as soon as possible. The anesthetic you received wears off quickly."

"I expected to be sick, too."

"The medications we use today don't usually cause the nausea and vomiting like they did in the past, but some people do get ill." As Alice's eyelids closed, Lori doubted if she would remember her explanation. Neither would Alice care that propofol was used more often than other agents for the reasons she'd indicated.

She finished her tasks and gave Alice's abdomen a quick peek before she left her in peace for a few minutes.

Without anything to occupy her mind, Lori's attention drifted to the clock. It was nearly nine-thirty—past time for Mac to have returned from Ronnie's school. Although she hadn't asked him, she'd hoped that he'd stop in and tell her how their morning had gone, but either he didn't think it important enough or he'd gotten sidetracked.

Surely he'd know that she'd be waiting for news, she

thought a trifle waspishly as she straightened the contents of the supply cabinet.

"Are we getting inspected today?" Talia asked from behind.

"Not that I know of."

"No famous person is coming through with a white glove?"

"No. Why do you ask?"

"Because I haven't seen you rearrange the shelves before. Something has obviously gotten you all aflutter." She gave a sly wink. "Or, should I say, some*one* has turned you into what my great-aunt would call a flibbertigibbet?"

Lori closed the cabinet door. "Today was Ronnie's breakfast at school."

Talia nodded. "I thought so. Didn't it go well?"

"That's just it. I don't know. I haven't seen Mac—Dr Grant," she corrected herself, "to ask."

"No news is good news."

The familiar saying didn't quell Lori's misgivings. "I know, but if it didn't turn out the way Ronnie wanted, I'm going to have one unhappy little girl this evening. She set her alarm extra early so I could French-braid her hair before I left. Ronnie had to have everything just right. You'd have thought she was going on a date."

Talia grinned. "To her, it probably was."

Actually, it was as much a special occasion for Lori as it was for Ronnie. The hours spent choosing the right outfit and fixing her daughter's hair had all been geared to impress the man who was coming. The excitement of waiting for his arrival and the thrill of seeing Mac in her living room, looking quite handsome in a tweed jacket, tan shirt and dark brown trousers, sent a shaft of envy through her.

She wanted to be the one going out with Mac.

It was just as well that her schedule hadn't allowed her to watch the two of them leave the house. Why put herself through that turmoil? Instead, she'd consoled herself by picturing Ronnie tripping beside him toward his car, wearing her fancy purple shirt and black stretch pants and acting like her dream had come true.

"I just don't want her to be disappointed. Reality doesn't always meet one's expectations."

"I'm sure she had a wonderful time. Just relax. What could have happened, anyway?"

Let me count the ways. Ronnie chattered like a magpie and, after being around his quiet son, Mac could easily have wanted to stuff a sock in her mouth. On occasion, she herself certainly did.

And then there was Ronnie's propensity to ask questions that shouldn't be asked. He'd probably be able to answer those like "Why is the sky blue?" or "Where do rabbits go in the winter?", but those weren't the ones that Lori feared.

The question of why Corey had lived with his aunt for two years instead of with his father worried Lori the most. Although she'd speculated on his reasons, she wouldn't put it past her curious daughter to quiz Mac about it. At least they would only have been together for an hour, and most of those sixty minutes would have been spent with other parents and children.

Lori drew a deep breath. "You're right. I'm making more of this than I should." She forced herself to relax, but Mac's arrival brought a fresh wave of tension. He'd replaced his street clothes with another cotton V-neck shirt and drawstring pants from his inexhaustible green wardrobe. It was as if the man she'd seen earlier had disappeared.

"Good morning," he addressed them politely. "I see Ratna got an early start."

Dr Ratna, an Indian gynecologist with a last name that no one tried to pronounce for fear of offending her, always started her schedule early. "I expect we'll get her next patient shortly," Lori said, signaling Talia with her eyes to give them a few minutes alone.

She liked working with Talia because the other nurse didn't need to have things spelled out in detail. Her wink and broad smile before she wiped the traces from her face indicated that she'd caught the hint. "Then I'd better get ready, hadn't I?" she said, moving to the opposite side of the room without waiting for a reply.

Surely Mac would take advantage of the moment to say something, *anything*, about the morning, but he didn't act interested in the subject that had weighed on her for the last hour and a half. She hated to mix personal and professional business, but she couldn't possibly wait for a commentary until she talked to Ronnie this afternoon. She'd explode with curiosity well before then.

"How did things go at school this morning?" she asked.

"Fine." He looked up from the chart in his hand. "How did you expect them to go?"

"Fine." She winced at repeating such a generic answer. "I was just wondering."

"Well," he said, lifting one powerful shoulder in a unconcerned shrug, "it was like you said. We went to school, ate donuts, drank juice and coffee, walked around the school and left."

Getting him to share information was like pulling a stubborn tooth. "That's it? Surely you did more than that."

The blank look in his eyes turned to amused understanding. "Ah-h, I see. You want a play-by-play account."

Yes, she wanted to shout. She'd been fretting over this big event in her daughter's life, an event that had tied her in knots and forced her to beg a total stranger to act as Ronnie's father, and he didn't consider the particulars important enough to mention. The way in which he'd phrased it made her feel like an over-protective—and nosy— mother.

Her face warmed. "Maybe not an instant replay," she

conceded, "but I'd appreciate a few details. So I know what to expect with Corey," she tacked on as an afterthought.

His slate-colored eyes sparkled as if he recognized her feeble excuse for what it was. "Of course. I didn't realize. Let's see. We walked to the car and I told her how pretty she looked."

She imagined Ronnie preening under his compliment and was glad that she'd taken the extra time to arrange Ronnie's hair.

"We also chatted about how she wants a puppy."

"We can't afford a dog," Lori said defensively. "Vaccinations, dog food, flea collars and haircuts—"

Mac held up one hand. "You don't have to convince me. Corey wants one, too. If Martha still lived with us, I'd consider owning a pet, but right now I don't think I could handle the extra worry. Anyway, where were we?"

"You were on your way to school."

"Ah, yes. We went to the gymnasium and stood in line with several other fathers and daughters. I'd tell you who we talked to, but I didn't know them. We did discuss the weather, though. It's been rather dry for this time of year."

His innocence seemed overdone. "You don't have to make fun," she said stiffly.

"I'm not," he protested. "I just hadn't realized how easy you were to tease."

And Lori hadn't realized that Mac knew how.

"Seriously, though, we visited like polite gentlemen and little ladies. After we finished, we went to the classroom, raved over everyone's perfect papers, neat handwriting and colorful artwork, and I left shortly after the first bell rang."

"Oh." Lori hesitated. "I'm glad everything turned out so well."

His expression softened. "Were you worried?"

"Not worried. Concerned. She'd built this up as a major event in her life and I didn't want her to be disappointed."

"I'm not sure what she thought would happen, but I

certainly enjoyed myself." He grinned. "If she needs help deciding on a career, though, I have an idea."

"You do?"

"A talk-show host," he answered promptly.

Lori's tension disappeared in a flash under the brilliance of his wide smile, and she giggled. "She's good at holding up her end of a conversation."

"And then some. Seriously, though, she's a delight. You've done an excellent job of raising her."

Lori was certain that her face matched the scarlet hue of her uniform. "Thank you."

"If you don't have any other questions, I believe I have a colon resection waiting for me."

"Sure." She waved her hand. "Sorry for the delay."

"For you, I don't mind," he replied before he disappeared through the swinging doors that lead to the surgical corridor.

Surprised by his jovial attitude, Lori watched him leave, too shocked to uproot her feet.

Talia joined her a minute later. "I couldn't help but overhear. It sounded as if they both had a good time this morning."

"I'd say so."

"And you were worried. I will say this, though. If you play your cards right, you won't have to borrow a father for Ronnie. You can give her one of her very own."

"Don't be ridiculous." Her objection sounded halfhearted even to her own ears. She hadn't realized until then how badly she'd wanted Mac to like her daughter as much as she liked his son. Logically, it didn't matter because their lives would only overlap for a few weeks, but if, by chance, things lasted longer...she wouldn't object.

"I'm not. I've never seen him act so friendly, much less unbend enough to crack a smile and make jokes. You're onto something, girl, so don't screw it up."

"I'm not *on*to *anything*," Lori protested as her cautious

nature quickly asserted itself. She'd seen the flash of masculine interest in his eyes, but Mac didn't seem ready for a relationship. It seemed futile to raise her hopes and see them crushed at a later date.

"We have—*had*—a mutual interest in our children's classroom activities," she continued. "In another week, we'll both be back to business as usual."

"Uh-uh." Talia shook her head. "I saw the gleam in his eye and heard his for-you-I-don't-mind comment. Dr Grant isn't as disinterested as you think. I'd bet my half-carat engagement ring on it."

"I hope you're prepared to lose it," Lori advised her.

Talia shook her head. "I won't. Wait and see."

Wait and see. Hardly, Lori thought as she returned to Alice's bedside to take another set of quarter-hourly vital signs. Even if she disregarded the shadows in Mac's eyes, the shadows that dared her to dispel them, she didn't need days to learn that they were like a pair of unmatched socks. It didn't matter that a mere smile and kind word could double her heart rate, or that his scent could make her imagine scenes that she had no business imagining.

No matter how much she might wish it otherwise, in two evenings she'd seen how they were two totally different people with two totally different sets of values and lifestyles. He hired housekeepers and drove a Lexus; she scrubbed her own bathroom and prayed for her Pontiac to last several more years. He was caviar and prime rib; she was tuna casserole and ground beef.

And that was that. Lori would force her feminine needs back into pre-Mac dormancy and rest in the knowledge of how happy she'd made her daughter.

And speaking of happy, she was about to have one *un*-happy patient.

"All right, Alice," she said. "I know you don't want to, but it's time for you to change positions. We can't have you settling like a rock in a rut."

"I don't mind," Alice mumbled.

"You'll get sore if you lie in the same position. Let's give it a try."

As she helped Alice shift her weight, she realized that her advice also applied to herself. Ronnie's request had shaken her out of her rut, and it would be interesting to see where the rock symbolizing her life landed when the dust finally settled.

The following Thursday, Veronica sat on the cement patio in the back yard and giggled as a black and red fuzzy caterpillar inched its way around a tuft of grass growing through the cracks. "Look at this, Corey," she said as she reached down to take the worm on her finger.

"Sweet," he pronounced, pushing up his glasses for a closer look. "You have a wooly bear tiger moth."

"I thought it was a caterpillar."

"It is. They're just called wooly bears because of their hair."

That was one thing she'd learned about Corey. He knew about a lot of stuff and, what was even better, he didn't make her feel dumb because she didn't know the same things he did. "Is this one going to be a butterfly?"

"He'll be a tiger moth," Corey corrected.

"When?"

"Next spring. Of course, that's if he lives through the winter. He's looking for a place to hibernate and then when it warms up again he'll eat for a while before he spins his cocoon. A few weeks later he'll be a moth."

"Wow. How did you know that?"

Corey held out his finger for the caterpillar to crawl on. "I read it in a book at the library."

"Did your dad take you?"

"Martha did. Dad was too busy." Corey glanced at Ronnie. "Your mom always has time for you."

"Yeah, I guess so. But your dad has a real important job, so maybe that's the difference."

"Maybe. He sure has to go to the hospital more." He paused. "I really like your mom."

"She's OK," Ronnie admitted, still smarting from the scolding she'd gotten for the dirty dishes she'd hidden under her bed. "Your dad is nice, too." Uncle Tim and her mother had told her many times how pretty she looked, but they didn't count.

"Does your mom tuck you in at night?"

"Sure. Doesn't your dad?"

"Martha usually did."

"Does he read you a bedtime story?"

"No."

"Gosh. I don't think I could go to sleep at night if my mom didn't do that."

"I listen to music," Corey offered.

Somehow, Ronnie didn't think it was quite the same, but she didn't want to hurt his feelings. "Maybe your dad doesn't know he's supposed to do that kind of stuff with you."

"Could be." Corey held his hand close to a stalk of dried grass so the caterpillar could go free. "We're interviewing more housekeepers this weekend. I don't want one."

"Why not?"

"'Cause I won't get to see Dad as often and I won't get to come here after school. I wish we could hire your mom. Do you think she'd want to work at my house instead of the hospital?"

Ronnie shook her head. "Don't think so. She likes taking care of sick people."

"I could be sick," he offered helpfully. "Once in a while."

"It wouldn't be the same."

"I know," he mourned. "She told me how hard she

worked to become a nurse because she'd always wanted to be one. I don't think she'd give it up for me.''

Ronnie was sad to see the caterpillar go. It reminded her of how she'd had to say goodbye to her friends when they'd moved here. If Corey got a housekeeper, she'd have to say goodbye to him, too. Sure, she'd see him at school, but it wouldn't be the same. She didn't like goodbyes.

''Wouldn't it be nice if we didn't have to borrow parents? They'd both be ours. Then you wouldn't need a housekeeper.''

''Yeah, but what can we do?''

''Well,'' Ronnie said as she thought of a plan, ''I asked your dad if he had a girlfriend and he said no. My mom doesn't have a boyfriend either, so there's no reason why we can't all live together.''

''They're not going to listen to us,'' Corey warned.

''Of course they won't. We're going to have to make them think it's their idea.''

''And how are we going to do that?''

Ronnie smiled. ''It's simple, really. I know they'd be happy together.'' Ronnie had seen a special smile on her mom's face when Dr Grant was there, when her mom thought no one was looking.

''How can you tell?''

Honestly! Boys could be so *dense* at times. ''Other parents don't usually hang around and visit with Mom when they pick up my friends. I think your dad is lonely.''

''He has me,'' Corey said, almost indignantly.

''He's lonely for a grown-up,'' Ronnie instructed him importantly. ''Someone who can stay up to watch the ten o'clock news and warm her feet at night.'' She'd heard her Aunt Molly tell her mom that the last time they visited, so it had to be right. Her mom always had cold feet whenever Ronnie crawled into her bed.

''What can we do?'' Corey asked. ''If Dad finds a housekeeper he likes…''

"You'll have to make sure that he doesn't," Ronnie informed him. "Can you do that?"

Corey's eyes gleamed with devilment, just like Alex's did before he got into trouble with their teacher, Mrs Cooper. "I think so."

"Good." She glanced over her shoulder to make sure her mother wasn't listening nearby. "Now, here's what we're going to do…"

CHAPTER FOUR

"WILL you be OK for a few minutes while I run to the pharmacy?" Talia asked on Friday morning, shortly after Lori had arrived from accompanying Corey to school. "The drug cabinet is nearly empty and because I'm on call this weekend, I'd like to restock it now."

"Good idea. Would you mind dropping off those empty blood bank units at the lab on your way?" Lori pointed to the counter near the doorway before she opened another box of syringes and refilled a drawer. She'd expected their first patients by now, but apparently the procedures hadn't gone quite as smoothly as anticipated. Until they arrived, she could find plenty of little jobs to keep herself busy.

Brad, who was standing at the counter, looked up from the chart in his hand. "Did I hear that you ladies need an errand boy?"

Lori grimaced at Brad's syrupy tone. She didn't know which she hated more—his overly friendly attitude or his grumpy mood. Either way, his temper seemed more mercurial than a high pressure system and she didn't feel like pandering to him today. Her time with Corey had given her a lot to think about, namely why Mac didn't take time to have fun and enjoy his son. Although she told herself to stay out of their affairs, Corey's need for love was hard to ignore.

"We need to pick up a few things," she told Brad, "but we can manage."

His smile was wide and, in Lori's opinion, somewhat fake. "You're both busy. I'll be happy to go."

"You were complaining earlier about the ton of paperwork waiting for you," Talia reminded him.

"Ah, but I need to stretch my legs."

Lori narrowed her eyes. Brad didn't do anything out of the goodness of his heart. "I don't buy the excuse of exercise, not after you've whined about how many miles you walk around here."

"All right," he said in his most long-suffering voice. "I hear we have a new pharmacist and I want to check her out."

Talia rolled her eyes. "Oh, brother."

"Hey," he protested. "I'm trying to make the new employee feel welcome."

Both women groaned.

Lori folded her arms. "I suppose if you do this for us, you'll grumble about how you have to do our work as well as yours."

He held up one hand. "I won't. Scout's honor."

"You weren't a Boy Scout," Talia accused.

Brad sniffed. "I was, too. Many years ago. You weren't even born yet."

"Not that old saw again." Lori thrust the sack of empty blood bags and the copies of the transfusion records at him. "Here. Have fun. And you'd better be back in thirty minutes. I want to take care of all the paperwork before this place turns into a zoo." The controlled drugs had to be carefully accounted for and stored under lock and key to meet federal requirements or heads would roll. She'd rather it wasn't hers.

"Your wish is my command." With a theatrical bow, he left.

Talia watched the doors swing closed behind him. "That guy is weird. One minute he's yelling at us over nothing and the next he's Mr Helpful."

"You never know what to expect from Brad," Lori agreed. "Although right now he's obviously trying to get on our good side. He probably thinks it's time for a little damage control because of my last incident report."

"I wonder what he has to do before anyone will clip his wings?"

Lori shuddered. "I don't want to think about it."

"You get along well with Dr Grant these days. Have you thought of saying something to him?"

"I did," Lori admitted, remembering their short conversation concerning Mr Clark.

"Really? When?"

"The day Dr Harrington had to take his patient back to surgery. You probably didn't notice because you were busy with your own patients."

"What did he say?"

"You mean, after he saw firsthand how Brad didn't give a charted dose?" At Talia's nod, Lori explained. "He asked me if this had happened before and I couldn't lie. I was afraid he'd dismiss it or try to excuse the mistake, but he didn't. Naturally, even though I brought it to his attention, I still filled out all the risk management forms. I can't believe that I haven't told you this before."

Talia shrugged. "We were busy that day."

"Anyway," Lori continued, "I assume he talked to Brad, because he's been on his toes the last few days, but we'll never know for sure. I'm certainly not going to ask Dr Grant if he counseled his employee, and Brad definitely won't broadcast it if he did. I'm hoping things will be better from now on."

"Amen to that," Talia said fervently.

The double doors burst open with a clang and Lori immediately shot to attention.

"We need suction here!" Mac and one of the circulating nurses ran alongside a gurney where the unmistakable sounds of retching were taking place.

Lori quickly flipped the switch to the wall unit and began suctioning the fluids out of the patient's mouth while the two nurses set the brakes. "Fifteen-year-old with an emergency appendectomy," Mac informed her over the slurping noise of the vacuum. "He tried to eat breakfast, but doubled over and collapsed on the floor of his kitchen. His parents brought him right in. They denied knowing he'd been ill."

"Was it ruptured?"

"Yeah." Mac's face was grim. "We started him on vancomycin during surgery. Get a peak level in thirty minutes."

The drug he'd mentioned was one of the most powerful antibiotics in a physician's arsenal, but receiving too much wasn't always a good thing. The dosage had to be carefully monitored to avoid toxicity.

"He was doing fine until we wheeled him into the hallway."

The young man, Blake Potter, hadn't been the first person who'd needed intervention while caught between surgery and the recovery room. Sometimes those few feet seemed as long as a mile.

"Watch him closely," Mac continued. "He doesn't need pneumonia on top of everything else."

"I will." The suction hose had remained empty, so Lori switched off the pump. She laid the hose on his bed for immediate access while she started the usual checks-and-numbers game. Blake still looked pale and she had a feeling that he'd require her full attention until his stomach settled.

"I'm cold," he mumbled.

"I'll get another blanket." Lori retrieved a blanket from the warmer designed for that express purpose and draped it over him. With winter coming on, she wished she had something similar at home.

Mac's pager sounded and he didn't waste any time in picking up the phone to dial the number. As soon as he identified himself, he listened, then said, "I'll be right there." After dropping the handset back in its cradle, he asked, "Questions?"

At Lori's negative head shake, he said, "I'm off to ER."

His scent hadn't cleared the air before another patient arrived, and then another.

"Another day in the fast lane," Talia said under her breath.

"Look on the bright side," Lori said as she ran her practiced eye over the blips and bleeps of the monitor screens. "The day will fly by."

For the next two hours, Lori dealt with Blake's nausea and the myriad tasks inherent with her job. She carefully monitored his drainage tubing, the bandage around the incision and the warmth of his toes. A call to the lab brought a technician to draw a blood sample at the appropriate time.

"Has Brad ever brought those meds to us?" Lori asked during a momentary lull.

Talia shook her head. "I didn't sign for them. Since you're asking, I assume you didn't either."

"Darn that man. It doesn't take two hours to travel from here to the pharmacy, the lab and back again. If he's been sweet-talking his new lady love all this time, I'm going to—"

"Here are your goodies," Brad said as he burst through the doors to place his cargo on the counter.

Lori raised one eyebrow. "Did you get lost?"

"I beg your pardon," he said, affronted. "ER paged me. Some big guy, a construction worker, fell off scaffolding on St Patrick's Church. It looks like he's broken his neck, among other things. ER wanted us to intubate him, but I didn't have any luck. We had to call out the big guns."

So that was the case in ER requiring Mac's presence. She hoped the situation wasn't as bad as Brad had indicated.

"That guy's a mess," Brad reported. "We're LifeWatching him out just as soon as the chopper gets here."

Omaha was the closest tertiary care facility and it wasn't

unusual for the helicopter service to make several runs a week.

"Anyway, I've got to go," he complained. "Can one of you take this stuff off my hands?"

"I'll do it." Lori compared the vials he'd brought against the paperwork, then locked everything away in the cabinet. "You're all set for the weekend, Talia."

"Let's hope I won't have to use any of it."

The rest of the day passed uneventfully. Because Lori had taken the late shift to accommodate her breakfast at school with Corey, the two children had walked home. When she arrived shortly after five, she found them in Ronnie's room, deeply engrossed in their Go Fish cards.

"Hi, guys," she said.

"Hi, Mom."

"Hi, Mrs Ames."

Lori noticed the juice boxes and the plate of cracker crumbs on the floor. "I see you had your snack."

"Uh-huh." Corey picked up another card from the discard pile.

"Have fun."

Lori left them to their game and hurriedly changed into more comfortable clothes. She couldn't wait to relax and sip on a cup of hot apple cider until dinnertime. Knowing she would run late today, she'd simmered chili in the crockpot and hoped that Mac would like it. In the space of their ten-day-old arrangement, he'd arrived in the middle of their meal on all but one occasion. He always stayed long enough to eat and it had become a routine to set a place for him at her table and to see his broad shoulders rising above the high-backed chair.

She hadn't realized how many special touches had gone by the wayside over the years with only Ronnie at home. With Mac's and Corey's regular appearances, she'd gradually reincorporated the little details of matching the stainless-steel cutlery, folding the napkins and using serving bowls instead of eating buffet-style from the stove. It felt good to add those small gestures again, although she convinced herself that she was only doing them to teach the children proper etiquette.

On this particular Friday, Mac arrived at five-thirty instead of six. Lines of exhaustion marred his handsome face and fatigue filled his eyes as if his week's stressful schedule had finally caught up to him.

"I'll fix a mug of cider while you let Corey know you're here," she told him. It had occurred to her that Mac and his son were virtual strangers because of Mac's profession, and her gift would be drawing them together. Of course, her success depended upon how long her influence lasted, but she could already see some changes in the way Mac looked at and treated his son. They both needed to form new habits where each other was concerned.

Lori went to the kitchen while Mac ambled down the hall to Ronnie's room.

"Hi, Dad," Corey said, flashing him a brilliant smile before he concentrated on the cards in his hand.

"Hi, son. Ronnie."

"Hiya, Dr Grant."

Mac studied the two children, who'd returned to their game. Corey had definitely thrived during his time here. He seemed happier and definitely more outspoken than before. Perhaps Martha had been right. Corey did need more than a grandmotherly figure in his life if he was ever to learn the dynamics of a family relationship. Unfortunately, Mac wasn't in any position to teach him and he couldn't prevail upon Lori to shoulder the task indefinitely.

Corey's voice stopped him from heading toward the kitchen. "Are we staying for dinner, Dad?"

"Do you want to?" he asked, hoping his son would agree and praying that he wouldn't. Staying here, even for an hour, was becoming as addictive as the alcohol he'd pickled himself with after Elsa had died. His awareness of

Lori had grown by leaps and bounds, although he'd taken great pains not to show it. A no-strings affair was all he was emotionally capable of offering, and so far he hadn't seen any signals to indicate she would welcome such an arrangement.

Once again it struck him as odd that he would even consider such a thing. For the past few years his career and son had filled his days to the max, although sadly Corey hadn't received his due. While he was now trying to balance those two responsibilities, in less than two weeks Lori had made him wonder if he might need something else as well. Something to round off the hard edges in his soul that medicine and a child couldn't touch. Something more personal, more intimate.

Corey's head bobbed like a cork in a tub of water. "It smells good, doesn't it?"

"Yes, it does," Mac agreed. After Martha had moved out, the only food smells in their house were the aromas left behind from their take-out boxes. He hated to feel beholden to Lori for their meals, too, but his stomach hadn't permitted him to refuse her kind and generous offer.

He'd make it up to her somehow.

Apparently taking Mac's response as an indication that they weren't going home yet, Corey returned to his cards. Mac smiled, feeling dismissed, but as he turned, the row of picture frames on the wall caught his attention.

Studio portraits of Ronnie at various ages hung at different heights, as well as two enlarged snapshots of Ronnie as a baby, being held in a man's arms. Obviously, the fellow was her father if the resemblance between him and the Ronnie of today was any indication.

What struck Mac closest to home was this fellow's body language. He looked as if he was afraid this wiry little bundle would explode at a moment's notice. Mac had the sneaking suspicion that after the photographer had snapped the shutter, Ronnie had been passed back to her mother.

It was almost like staring in a mirror.

The snapshot Mac kept in his drawer under his socks, the same snapshot that had been taken six months after Elsa's death, showed Mac wearing the same uncomfortable expression as Ronnie's father. He knew why he looked as he did, but what was Lori's husband's excuse?

"I see you found my daughter's photo gallery." Lori smiled at him as she handed the mug over with the handle facing him. "She was quite the photogenic little pixie."

"She still is. Is that her dad?"

Lori sipped her cider as she glanced past his finger. "Yes. Glenn was always nervous about holding her. He had this horrible fear of dropping her, which was silly since she was eighteen months old at the time. It shows, doesn't it?" Her chuckle sounded forced.

"I'm sure he got over it."

"No, he didn't. He died shortly after."

"I'm sorry. Car accident?"

"Supposedly."

He stared at her, surprised by her response. "You don't think so?"

She turned toward the kitchen and he followed. "He was definitely killed in a car wreck," she said as she scooped bank statements and bills into a pile. "I just don't think it was an accident."

"Suicide?"

"No. Glenn had problems and I suppose if he'd ever kept his doctor's appointments, he would have been diagnosed as manic-depressive, but suicide?" She shook her head. "His biggest problem was that he owed a lot of money to a lot of people and they weren't all reputable, if you know what I mean."

"Loan sharks?"

"Among others. But they weren't the only ones. As I was sorting through his business papers, I discovered several credit cards that I didn't know we had, charged to the max. The worst blow was the shoe box filled with IOUs to friends, relatives, his co-workers." She shrugged as she placed the pile of documents inside a drawer. "I have no idea where the money went. Gambling, I suppose."

"You didn't know what he was doing?"

"I had my doubts about where his money came from because he always had plenty, but whenever I asked, he had a plausible excuse. Overtime, a side job, whatever. I didn't want to think otherwise, so I accepted what he said at face value. After he died, I realized that he'd told me what I'd wanted to hear." She paused. "I paid the price for burying my head in the sand and, believe me, I don't intend to do it again."

"What did you do?" he asked, anticipating her answer.

"The only thing I could do. I finished my nursing degree, found a job and began fighting my way out of debt."

"You could have taken out bankruptcy."

Her smile was wan. "My pride wouldn't let me. Anyway, we managed. I found a credit counselor and he helped me budget my income so I could pay back my school loans, the financial companies and everyone else. I drew the line, though, at repaying the shady characters. Anyway, barring any unforeseen expenses, my slate will be clean in three or four years."

She rubbed her neck and shrugged as if she didn't have a care in the world, but he saw through her pretense. Her hands trembled slightly and she gazed at his chin rather than his eyes in her effort to shield the suspicious glimmer in those dark depths.

Mac reached out to hold her, but it had been so long since he'd comforted anyone that he stopped himself. In spite of feeling awkward, he couldn't deny the urge to touch her hair and stroke the side of her cheek. "It hasn't been easy, has it?"

Lori's gaze met his. To his surprise and relief, she pressed his hand against her face, and for several delightfully long seconds he soaked in everything about her—the smooth texture of her skin, the floral scent surrounding her, the silky feel of her hair against his arm. He hated to hear of her struggles, but her story only confirmed what he'd suspected.

"Let me pay you for your time with Corey," he said impulsively.

The mood instantly shifted. She stiffened, dropped his hand and stepped back. "I don't need your charity."

"This isn't charity," he insisted.

"Do you pay the parents of Corey's other friends when he visits?"

"Well, no..."

She crossed her arms. "I rest my case."

"I only want to do what's right and fair for you."

"If I didn't like this arrangement, I wouldn't have made it."

He'd already known she was proud and now he could add stubborn to the list. Then again, if obstinacy hadn't been an integral part of her character, she wouldn't have come as far as she had.

Mac held up both hands. "OK. I won't say another word about it."

"Good."

He shifted the focus of their conversation to defuse the tense moment and to clarify a few details. "You must have been a child bride if you have an eight-year-old daughter."

"In a manner of speaking. I was eighteen when I got pregnant with Ronnie and once that happened, we decided to get married. Looking back, we shouldn't have tied the knot, but it seemed the right thing to do at the time. What about you?"

He hadn't spoken of Elsa for years, but he couldn't expect Lori to share her past if he wasn't willing to reciprocate.

"I met Elsa in college. We knew from our first date that

we were meant to be together." His throat tightened and he drank his cider.

"That soon?"

"Oh, yes. She was gorgeous. Not just outside, but inside, too. She was sweet, loving, funny, and it seemed as if she could read my thoughts, my moods. We were definitely on the same wavelength."

"You were fortunate."

"I was," he admitted. "We got married in an elaborate affair before I entered medical school. She was a teacher, so she didn't have any trouble finding a job. Everyone, especially her students, loved her. She was my whole life. My reason to get up in the morning."

The familiar maudlin feeling was starting to descend and he willed it away. "She'd been advised not to get pregnant because she was a severe diabetic and had a heart defect, so we decided to adopt as soon as I finished my residency."

"Best-laid plans," she murmured.

"Exactly. The doctor advised her to terminate the pregnancy, but she refused. Things went better than we'd expected and we both started to feel as if everything would work out. As much as we loved each other, how could it not?"

He paused, waiting for the familiar pain to clutch his gut and close off his throat, but to his surprise he felt more sadness than heart-wrenching sorrow. "Toward the end, everything that could have gone wrong did. Then, during labor, she developed an amniotic embolism and died. I felt utterly helpless. Here I was, a physician, with the staff of an entire obstetrics department at my disposal, and I couldn't do a thing."

"You must have been devastated."

"To put it mildly. My life, which had been perfectly on track, had turned upside down in a few hours."

"Leaving you with a baby."

He leaned against the counter and stared into the cloudy

liquid in his cup. "I couldn't stand the thought of having this helpless infant instead of Elsa."

"So you blamed Corey."

He nodded. "Like my in-laws blamed me. They refused to keep in contact, so I sent Corey to my sister's and finished my training. For a while, I turned to alcohol, but it didn't take long to realize that drinking in my spare time wasn't the solution. My profession became my crutch instead."

"What turned things around?"

"Six months after I finished my residency, my sister brought Corey back. She didn't want to, but she told me that his place was with me." He managed a weak grin. "She suggested that I stop working twenty-hour days and start living again now that I had a two-year-old depending on me."

Lori smiled. "In other words, think about getting married."

"How did you guess?"

"My sister tells me the same thing. Obviously, though, you didn't."

He shook his head. "I hired a nanny for the first few years."

"And kept your same hectic schedule."

Mac shrugged. "At first, I couldn't bear to come home—the nanny wasn't Elsa. By the time I got over those feelings, I'd made myself indispensable at the hospital. I *couldn't* come home whenever I wanted because I had patients depending on me. Anyway, when my nanny quit, I found Martha."

"You were lucky."

"I was. I hope my next housekeeper can compare."

"Actually, I was thinking of you and your wife. Not everyone gets the opportunity to share a love that's so special. Even if it didn't last the fifty or sixty years you'd planned, at least you were able to experience it for a little while."

Her comment jolted him out of his melancholy mood. "Is that how you felt about your marriage?"

She stared at the floor tiles for a few seconds before she met his gaze. "No. If Ronnie hadn't come along, we would have gone our separate ways long before we discussed weddings. He was having a tough time with his personal life and I felt sorry for him. Glenn said that he needed me and I was flattered and naïve enough to think that I could save him from himself.

"My parents weren't pleased by my decision, so we said our vows before a judge at the courthouse. My sister, Molly, and I baked a cake for our friends—that was the extent of our celebration."

She heaved a deep breath. "So, no, I didn't experience what you did in more ways than one. I'll always regret missing out."

"It could still happen."

"Maybe, maybe not. I know one thing, though, if I'm fortunate enough to have a second chance, I won't settle for anything less than what you had."

"I guess that's where we're different," he said slowly. "Even if I were willing, no other relationship could compare to what I had with Elsa. Not only that, but I refuse to go through that pain again."

During those moments when the house was quiet and Ronnie was fast asleep across the hall, Lori had imagined a man like Mac filling those empty places inside her. Although she didn't hold out any great hope for it to happen, hearing him plainly state that no other woman could measure up to his wife completely destroyed her fantasy.

Lori would have liked to have argued the point, to tell him that isolating himself wasn't healthy, but he spoke as if his mind was made up and nothing she could say would change it. So she didn't try.

He probably didn't mean his rejection to be personal, but it certainly seemed so. Even without Mac's description, she assumed Elsa had been as beautiful as her name—and a veritable saint—and Lori was, well, just Lori. She was the invisible girl-next-door, the behind-the-scenes gal who kept things running smoothly so that everyone else could enjoy themselves.

Thank goodness she hadn't done anything foolish when he'd tried to comfort her. As it was, she'd probably let him see far more than he should have when she'd pressed his hand to her face. He'd never know how badly she'd wanted to feel his arms around her, because she didn't want to strain their newlyformed friendship. He clung to his past love like a man hanging on a lifeline, and any perceived threat would only cause him to grip it tighter. He'd told her things that few others knew, and she didn't want to jeopardize their fragile connection.

At least she understood why a chasm separated Mac from his son and why Mac was determined to remain single. Just as he anesthetized his patients against physical discomfort, he'd anesthetized himself to emotional pain by sealing off his heart.

Fortunately, Mac's attitude toward Corey had changed and he was willing to modify his parenting ways, at least as far as his job would allow. If only she could ensure that he wouldn't slide back into his old habits, regardless of his good intentions, once he hired the next housekeeper.

"Please, don't be angry with me for saying this," she began, "but Corey needs someone more permanent in his life than a person who stays until they receive a better job offer."

"He has me."

"Yes, he does, but I'm worried more about what will happen when you find another Martha. Will you go back to spending your days and nights at the hospital? Will he take second place again?"

"At times, it's going to be unavoidable," he said defensively. "I'd like to promise that I'll be home every night, but I can't. My branch of medicine isn't a nine-to-five job."

"It's not a question of once in a while," she pressed on, determined to be Corey's advocate. "I understand about sharing the on-call schedule. I'm just curious if you intend to cover the department by yourself." *Like you did before*, she thought. In spite of having one partner and five CRNAs, Mac had pencilled his name on the calendar more often than not.

"As the one who is ultimately responsible for the entire service, I'm *expected* to put in more hours than everyone else, especially when there's no one else to call upon."

"Yes, but—"

"For the record, Josh and I are trying to make things more equitable, but it's going to take time. Corey has to understand that and be patient."

"I'm sure he is," she began.

"I also realize we aren't as close as we could be," he admitted. "While our quantity of time together isn't the same as what you and your daughter share, I'm trying to improve the *quality*. For now, it's the best I can do."

Lori felt duly chastised at his sharp tone. "I'm sorry," she said stiffly. "I had no right to say anything. I just want Corey to be happy."

His shoulders heaved with a sigh as if he regretted his outburst. He rubbed his face with one hand and when he spoke again, his voice was even. "Speaking of happy, Ronnie wants a father. Are you going to give her one?"

She hadn't expected him to turn the tables. "When I find the right guy, she'll have the father she's always wanted. Until then, we'll manage on our own."

Once again, a pregnant pause descended until a girlish voice interrupted from the doorway. "Is it time to eat?"

Saved by a child, Lori thought, grateful for always-hungry children. "It certainly is," she said with a counterfeited heartiness. "By the time you two wash your hands, I'll have dinner on the table."

Unfortunately, she'd lost her appetite. She could only hope that she hadn't lost her opportunity to look out for Corey's interests as well.

CHAPTER FIVE

"Thanks for coming, Mrs Spillman," Mac said as he ushered his latest applicant to the door. "I'll get back to you in a few days."

Hattie Spillman, a spry woman in her sixties, smiled benevolently at Corey. "I'll be looking forward to your call. I did tell you that I'll be gone Monday for the bank's historic home tour."

"Yes, you did."

"And I mentioned that Tuesday morning is my bridge club."

"Yes," Mac said. "I remember."

"Did I say something about needing Friday afternoons off for my weekly trip to the beauty shop?"

Mac struggled to keep from staring at her white hair, which looked as if she'd walked through a wind tunnel. "No, I don't believe you did."

"Oh, my. I'd lose my head if it wasn't attached. The mind isn't as sharp as it used to be." Her hands fluttered to the wisps hanging on her forehead. "Well, I couldn't bear to lose my standing appointment with Carlton for a shampoo and set. Why, I know a woman who's been on his waiting list for *years*. I'd be *devastated* if he gave my time slot to someone else."

Mac opened the door. "We certainly wouldn't want to be responsible for upsetting your routine."

"How thoughtful. I wish my grandchildren felt the same. Did I mention that I have three?"

"Yes, you did." Mac had the niggling suspicion that Corey would be the one looking after Hattie, instead of the other way around.

She bent down to tweak Corey's cheek. "Such a delightful little boy. You won't be any trouble at all, will you?"

"No ma'am," Corey answered dutifully, although Mac could see the resentment shining in his eyes and tense line to his jaw as she pinched his skin with vigor. In the last two weeks, Mac had learned to read Corey as only a parent could, which had been rather enlightening. He'd never thought of Corey being particularly stubborn, but he'd seen evidence of it more often than he'd expected. Either Corey had matured to the point where he wanted more independence, or Mac had finally spent enough time with his son to see what had been under his nose all these years.

He suspected it was the latter.

In any event, Mrs Spillman needed to go because their chores were waiting. He and Corey had to spend what was left of their Sunday afternoon doing laundry and he wanted to catch up on a few back issues of *The Anesthesiologist* before playing the promised game of checkers.

Mac shook off his thoughts and bestowed a polite smile upon their guest. "As I said, I'll be in touch."

She stepped over the threshold. "I'll be gone on Monday."

"I won't forget," he promised as he started to close the door. "Goodbye."

As soon as the latch clicked, Mac heaved a sigh, then glanced at Corey. "What did you think of her?" he asked.

Corey peered at him owlishly through his glasses. "Do you have to ask, Dad?"

Mac smiled as he gently caressed the red mark on Corey's cheek. Where had the baby he remembered gone? It wouldn't be long before Corey would be driving, shaving and, heaven forbid, dating. How could he possibly navigate those choppy waters without Elsa? Out of habit, he searched Corey's face for traces of her and waited for the familiar stab of pain to hit on recognition. To his surprise, the eyes, the nose, the high cheekbones that he'd associated with his wife weren't hers. They were Corey's—a unique blend of both his parents.

It was a startling revelation, and one he wasn't totally comfortable with, because he didn't know what it meant. In fact, he wasn't sure that he *wanted* to know.

"Dad?"

Mac pulled himself back to the present. "Sorry. Does it hurt?"

"A little."

"Want an ice pack?"

"It's not that bad. I'm OK." He cocked his head. "I hear the dryer buzzing."

"Then we'd better take care of it, hadn't we?" Mac replied.

A few minutes later, as Corey watched him fold his jeans, he asked, "Are you going to cross Mrs Spillman off your list?"

Mac smiled at Corey's hopeful expression. "I'd say so. What did you think about Mrs Partridge?"

Corey grimaced. "I didn't like the bird lady."

"Bird lady?"

"Yeah. Partridge. Bird. Get it?"

"Ah, the bird lady. Well, I wouldn't call her that to her face."

"I'll bet her students did," Corey said, clearly convinced. "She even looks like a bird with her pointy nose and beady eyes."

Mac saw the resemblance, but he was slowly running out of applicants. Perhaps it was time to focus on their good points rather than the bad ones. "Yes, but she could help you with your homework."

"But did you hear her, Dad? She said the school curriculum has gone downhill since she left and that she's going to make sure I learn everything I need to know. I don't want to go to school when I get home." Corey crossed his arms as a mulish set appeared on his face.

Of the three, Mrs Partridge was by far the best, but Mac had promised Corey that he wouldn't hire anyone who wasn't mutually agreeable. Perhaps he'd spoken too soon. He hadn't dreamed that finding someone would be this difficult. In the past, he hadn't interviewed more than three ladies before he'd found one who'd been suitable.

"What about Belinda Fabrizio?"

Corey shook his head emphatically. "She spent all her time looking at you and asking what your schedule was. I don't think she even noticed me."

Belinda was a single woman in her mid-twenties. Her sultry smile and the way she batted her mascara-coated eyelashes had made him decidedly uncomfortable. He didn't doubt for a second that hiring Ms Fabrizio would cause more trouble than she was worth, but if Corey had liked her, then he would have gritted his teeth and borne it.

By staying away from home again? For a moment, he wasn't sure if his own conscience had been speaking, or if somehow, Lori could project her thoughts.

"I think you're right," Mac admitted. "So she's out of the running."

"Good. Then we'll just have to keep looking."

Mac saw a trace of satisfaction flit across Corey's face and suddenly he knew without having a Ph.D. in psychology that he was being manipulated.

"You know, son, we can't keep going like we have been."

"Why not? Don't you want to spend time with me any more?"

Mac inwardly winced at his son's assessment of the situation. "It's not that I don't want to stay home with you. I have responsibilities at the hospital." He thought of the work in his briefcase, waiting for his attention after Corey had gone to bed.

"But you're the boss, Dad. You should deli—dela—" He paused. "There's a word for it. It means when you give your jobs to other people so you don't have to do them yourself."

"Delegate?"

"That's it."

"And where did you hear that?" Mac asked, although he had his suspicions.

"From our teacher, Mrs Cooper. It's one of our spelling words this week."

Mac felt a little guilty for assuming that Lori might be undermining his efforts to find a housekeeper. She only had Corey's best interests at heart. As determined as she was to draw the two of them closer, she wouldn't pit his son against him.

"The point is," he began as he folded the final pair of jeans, "we need help with the chores around here. Wouldn't you rather we did fun things instead?"

"I don't mind," Corey said loyally. "And I *like* going to Lori's every afternoon."

Mac did, too. "I know you do, but Lori is looking after you as a favor to me. It isn't fair to impose on her indefinitely."

"She doesn't mind. She *enjoys* having us over. I know because she said so."

"Yes, but we don't take advantage of our friends," he said, feeling like a parent as he delivered his words of wisdom. "We need to find someone to live here so we can get back to our routine. I adjusted the call schedule for this month, but next month is a different story."

Corey's lower lip trembled and he sounded resigned. "You're going to work all the time again, aren't you?"

"No," Mac corrected him. "I promise my schedule won't be like it was before, but I'll have to cover a few more days than I do now. It will be easier on both of us if we find a housekeeper." The laundry alone had become a task of monumental proportions. He couldn't comprehend how the two of them managed to wear so many clothes.

"But, Dad," Corey protested, "we have a routine *now*."

"Our current arrangement was only meant to be temporary," Mac reminded his son gently. "You knew that."

Panic rose in Corey's eyes. "You promised that you wouldn't hire anyone unless I liked her."

"Yes, but—"

Corey squared his stance as he balled his hands into fists at his side. "You promised."

"I fully intend to keep that promise," Mac said, hating the position in which he'd placed himself. "But you have to work with me here. You've met ten ladies and found something wrong with every one."

Corey relaxed a little. "You didn't like them either."

The sad thing was, Corey was right. Mac had found some small detail about each that had prevented him from hiring them on the spot, although he could accept either Mrs Partridge or Mrs Racine. Strangely enough, choosing them made him feel as if he were settling for second best. Was he asking for too much when he wanted someone who was kind, loving, thoughtful, had a sense of humor, liked children and knew how to run a house and juggle their differing schedules smoothly?

"Besides," Corey continued, "I'm going to spend the most time with this person so I should have the final say."

Mac wondered if children had an innate sense of knowing how to send their parents on a guilt trip, or if they learned the skill in school from their peers.

"I realize that," he said. "But no matter which woman we hire, we're going to go through an adjustment period until we get to know each other."

Corey's mulish expression hadn't disappeared and Mac felt compelled to appease him as much as possible. "What are you looking for? We're not going to find another Martha, you know."

"I don't want another Martha." Before Mac could ask

him to explain, Corey volunteered the information. "I want someone like Lori."

Corey's wish didn't come as any great surprise. For the past week, his son had sung her praises. Mac couldn't blame him. He enjoyed his time with her, too, even when she fearlessly spoke her opinion. She'd only been looking out for Corey and he couldn't fault her for that.

Perhaps he hadn't been thrilled with any of the applicants because he, too, had set Lori as the standard. In comparison, each one fell extremely short. Those few hours spent at her house each evening had become an important part of his day and he knew that coming home to a meal prepared by a housekeeper simply wouldn't be the same.

"Why can't we hire Lori?"

"She has a job."

"I know, but can't you fire her at the hospital?"

Mac smiled. "I'm not her supervisor."

"Oh." Corey sank onto the sofa, and although he didn't say anything Mac could see the wheels of thought turning. "Do you like Lori?" he asked.

"Yes, I do."

"A lot?"

Far more than he should, but Mac bit back the comment. "She's a very nice woman."

"Couldn't you just marry her? Then Ronnie would have a dad, I would have a mom, we wouldn't need a housekeeper and none of us would be lonely."

Marry Lori? The idea wasn't as frightening as he'd expected, but it was still out of the question. "I don't want to get married."

"Why not?"

"Because..." His mind raced with excuses before he decided that Corey was old enough to understand the truth. "Because I loved your mother very much and I'm not interested in getting married again."

"Aunt Liz says you should. It's not good for you to be alone so much."

"Aunt Liz says a lot of things. And, anyway, I'm happy with my life the way it is. Aren't you?"

The silence was deafening. Obviously Corey wasn't as satisfied as Mac wanted him to be.

"Things here aren't so bad, are they?" Mac pressed.

"No, but they'd be even better if Lori was my mom," Corey countered.

Unable to dispute that argument, Mac simply placed the pile of jeans in Corey's arms and changed the subject. "As soon as you put your clothes away, we'll play checkers."

"OK." Corey sounded resigned, rather than excited.

By the time Mac had set the board out on the kitchen table, Corey had returned. It soon became obvious as Mac captured piece after piece that Corey's mind wasn't on the game and Mac knew why.

"It's going to work out," he reassured him. "Things won't be as bad as you think."

Corey didn't appear convinced. "Sure, Dad," he said politely, *too* politely. "Can we finish this later?"

"Would you rather play something else?"

"Nah. I think I'll just go upstairs."

Their camaraderie had disappeared, but Mac didn't want to give up so easily. "If you have homework, you could bring it into my office so we can work together."

"I finished it yesterday. I just want to do stuff in my room."

Alone wasn't stated, but the implication couldn't have been more plain. A door had slammed between them and Mac was powerless to keep it open. As he watched his son trudge away, Mac offered another suggestion. "Let's shoot a few hoops when it stops raining."

The excitement he'd expected to see didn't appear. "Sure, Dad. Whatever."

If Mac heard "Sure, Dad' one more time, he was going

to explode. He was almost tempted to call his sister for advice, but he knew what she'd say.

Get a life, Mac. Elsa died, but you didn't.

Why did people think they knew what he needed better than he did? It grew tiresome to hear the same advice sung over and over again, no matter how many different tunes his family used. It was only bearable because Mac knew they meddled out of love and concern.

Ignoring the pile of sheets and towels awaiting his attention, he sought sanctuary in his office, although here the gloomy mood hovered as strongly as it did throughout the rest of the house. Normally, he didn't notice the overcast sky or the patter of raindrops against the window, but today he did.

He settled behind his desk and picked up the first magazine, only to discover how unappealing the article on current anesthetics awaiting FDA approval was. After tossing it back on the pile in disgust, he closed his eyes and visualized the days when he and his sister Liz had been trapped indoors by the weather.

They would occupy themselves with whatever board games were at hand and when they tired of those and started squabbling over whose turn it was to choose the next activity, his father would intervene.

He never knew how his dad had managed the feat of pulling something special out of the closet because Mac had kept his eyes open for unusual packages stashed at the back. Invariably, his father would bring out a model of some sort and they would spend the next few hours building an airplane, a car or a train. By the time they finished, his mother would bring in a plate of cookies or brownies. *For the builders*, she would say before she dutifully admired whatever project Liz and he had completed.

Ironically, he wondered what Corey would remember when he reached Mac's age. Would he remember the checker games and last night's water fight as they'd washed their breakfast dishes? Would he recall the time they'd popped popcorn in the microwave and burned it? Or would Corey simply think of a solitary pursuit performed in the privacy of his room? Somehow, he doubted if Ronnie logged many hours alone. No doubt she was at this very moment cuddled on the sofa with Lori, reading a book or sitting on the floor engrossed in a rousing hand of Old Maid.

He smiled, remembering how Lori had played cards with the two children and had looked as if she'd enjoyed herself as much as they had. Mac would never forget the happiness on his son's face as he'd passed the Old Maid card to Lori.

Couldn't you just marry her?

The objections he'd given Corey were still legitimate yet, from a logical standpoint, the idea definitely had merit. The truth was, Mac found Lori extremely attractive and enjoyed being in her company. The four of them got along well and, while marriage would be advantageous to him and Corey, Lori and Ronnie would reap benefits as well. Ronnie would have the father she wanted and Lori wouldn't have to struggle financially. In fact, she wouldn't have to work at all if she chose not to.

He wasn't ready to replace Elsa, which meant that any marriage would be a business arrangement centered on meeting a mutual need. While he could live with that, he didn't think Lori would embrace the concept. She wanted the marriage that she hadn't had before—one of undying love, romance and roses; one where someone loved her with every fiber of his being. Could he convince her to settle for something less, something along the lines of friendship and respect?

Somehow, he doubted it. She'd seemed rather adamant when she'd discussed her vision of a future relationship. Yet the possibility of Lori as his wife sent an urge to kiss her sweeping through him, along with a strong desire to hear her musical laughter. For him, her smile would turn this rainy day into one seemingly filled with sunshine.

Before he changed his mind, he strode toward Corey's room and knocked briskly to warn of his interruption. Corey shifted his attention from his half-finished cartoon drawing to him as Mac poked his head inside.

"What do you think about taking Ronnie and Lori to the movies?"

Corey's eyes lit up. "Can we?"

"I'll call and ask if they're free."

Corey shot to his feet, his drawing forgotten. "I bet they are. Ronnie says she doesn't get to do much on account of how much stuff costs."

No wonder Lori spent a lot of time playing games and going to the library. Now that he thought about it, he never saw Lori eating in the cafeteria. She always ate an apple or a carton of yogurt in the lounge.

"Hurry up, Dad," Corey said, his comment about the Ameses' finances clearly forgotten in his excitement. "The number is on the pad by the phone in the kitchen."

To Mac's amusement, Corey stuck to his side while he walked to the kitchen and spoke to Lori. "Corey and I want to know if you two ladies would be interested in a movie this afternoon."

Lori's chuckle was like a soothing balm to his soul. "It's a good idea, but our theater isn't showing anything appropriate for two eight-year-olds," she told him. "Is Corey having an attack of cabin fever, too?"

"Yeah. Too bad about the movie, though."

Corey's high spirits visibly deflated and Mac hated to see his high spirits fall.

"We could rent a movie instead," she suggested. "I've got popcorn."

Mac gratefully accepted her offer. The second he hung up, Corey jumped off the barstool. "What are we doing, Dad?"

"We're picking out a movie at the video store and watching it at their house."

Corey clapped his hands. "Oh, boy, oh, boy. This is gonna be so neat. I know just the one to get." He raced to the row of coat pegs on the wall separating the kitchen from the garage and fidgeted while Mac looked for his car keys. "Come on, Dad," he said impatiently. "Let's go."

Mac smiled. "Hold on. I'm coming."

Thirty minutes later, with a tape about an underdog kids' baseball team in hand, Mac raced Corey to Lori's front porch. After hearing his son's "Last one to the door is a rotten egg", he'd sprinted through the downpour, careful to stay a half-step behind. Hearing Corey's laughter was worth the price of getting soaked.

Lori watched Mac's car park in her driveway, feeling as excited as Ronnie acted, although she worked hard not to show it. She opened the door as soon Mac and Corey reached the relative protection of the porch and welcomed them inside.

Raindrops glistened like diamond chips in Mac's hair and she offered him a towel. "You two shouldn't need a bath tonight."

"Probably not," Mac agreed as he dried off. "I appreciate your invitation. Corey was a little down in the dumps and I thought an excursion would raise his spirits."

Lori glanced at the youngster who was deep in a discussion with Ronnie at the television. "He seems OK now."

"You should have seen him an hour ago. He didn't care for any of our three job applicants and he was upset when I mentioned how we had to make a decision within a few weeks."

"Why the time limit?" she asked, curious. "Wouldn't you rather wait until you found the right person for the job?"

"I can't," he said flatly. "I juggled this month's call schedule, but next month's is another story."

"Why?"

"Several people are scheduled for vacations and, to be honest, I can't keep up with the housekeeping details. It's only a matter of time until we're wearing pink underwear."

A vision of Mac in pink briefs made her smile. "Don't mix your reds and whites and you should be OK."

"That's easier said than done. And why is it that socks always lose their mates in the wash?"

Lori shrugged. "It's a fact of nature."

"Yeah, but I still can't wait to have a routine again."

Lori felt sorry for Corey as once again the routine he'd adjusted to would change. In her heart, she suspected that he wasn't as eager to embrace it as Mac was. For herself, she'd known their current arrangement was only a temporary measure, but it troubled her to hear it would soon end. Still, it was Sunday and those problems, along with her worries over her dwindling bank account, could wait for another day.

Lori claimed a seat on the sofa next to Mac in order to see the small television screen. His sleeve brushed against her arm from time to time and the scent of his aftershave mingled with the buttery aroma of the popcorn.

She'd never eat popcorn again without being reminded of MacKinley Grant.

Within minutes of the movie starting, a huge clap of thunder startled her and she sent a handful of popped corn flying toward him.

"I'm so sorry," she said, embarrassed by her reaction to the storm.

"I'm just glad you didn't have something heavier in your hand. I might have been injured for life." He grinned as he picked a kernel off his shirt and popped it into his mouth.

"Uh-oh, Mom," Ronnie said. "Corey spilled his drink."

"I'm sorry, Lori," Corey said, his eyes wide with worry. "I didn't mean to make a mess on your carpet. I tried to be real careful, but—"

"Accidents happen," Lori said as she hurried to fetch several towels to mop up the disaster. "I guess I'm not the only one who doesn't like thunder."

Sensing how flustered he was, Lori tried to put him at ease. "This is nothing," she told him. "I once made a cake for a friend's baby shower. It was one of those four-layer creations that took hours to make and I'd decorated it with fancy frosting and raspberries and such. I was so-o-o careful when I slid it into my cake carrier because I didn't want to bump a single frosting rose or raspberry."

His eyes were filled with interest rather than the shame she'd seen earlier, which told her that she'd taken his mind off his own clumsiness. "Anyway," she continued, "I was carrying it inside the building and I didn't see a step. I tripped, and do you know what?"

"What?" he asked, enraptured.

"This cake did the most perfect Olympic-style somersault you could ever see."

"Ooh," Corey gasped. "Did you catch it?"

Lori shook her head. "Nope. It landed upside down. Mind you, it hadn't fallen out of the carrier so it was edible, but my work of art wasn't a pretty sight."

"What did you do?" he asked.

"The only thing I could do. I scraped off all the mangled roses and crushed raspberries and tried to re-frost it. Believe me, my poor cake didn't look anything like it did before."

"I'll bet it still tasted good," Corey said, clearly loyal.

"It did, and you know what? My slip gave everyone a good laugh because, you see, we've all had this happen at one time or another." She gave the carpet one final swipe. "There. Good as new."

After tossing her wet towels on the washing machine in

the utility room, she rejoined Mac on the sofa while Ronnie restarted the movie.

Mac leaned closer so that his breath tickled her ear as he spoke. "What an interesting story."

She smiled as she shrugged off his thanks. "We all have our moments."

"Is it true?"

She leaned back and pretended horror. "Why, Dr Grant. Would I tell a tall tale to an impressionable child?"

His eyes crinkled with obvious merriment and it struck her how she'd never tire of seeing his grin or the dimple it revealed. He didn't show either often enough as far as she was concerned. "I think you would if it would make someone feel better," he whispered back.

"Rest easy," she told him. "Every word I said was true."

"When do you have time to bake fancy cakes?"

"I don't. Only for special occasions and only for my friends."

Ronnie turned around. "Shh, Mom. We can't *hear*."

"Sorry." She exchanged a smile with Mac but didn't say another word.

Ten minutes later, another huge clap of thunder reverberated through the house seconds after lightning had flashed. This time, the overhead lights flickered before the power went out.

Both Ronnie and Corey groaned. "Just when we were getting to a good part."

"I'm sure the electricity will come back on in a few minutes," Lori said. "Be patient."

The rain beat against the roof hard enough to make speech impossible. Five minutes later, Lori was afraid their power outage might last longer than she'd expected.

"Everybody stay where you are while I find some candles," she said. She stuck out her hand to feel her way and she touched a warm, solid chest when there should have been air.

Lori gasped and pulled back her hand.

"It's only me," Mac said with a distinct chuckle in his voice. "Do you have a flashlight?"

"Yes," she said, willing her heart rate to more normal levels, "but I'm not sure if the batteries might be flat."

"I have one in my car. I'll get it."

"Wait," she told him. "By the time I light the candles, the electricity will come on. It happens every time."

She fumbled her way to the kitchen and found the box of matches on top of the refrigerator. A flash of lightning lit her path back to the living room where she kept three decorative candles. A stroke of a match later, they'd chased most of the darkness into the corners.

"We're all set," she said brightly.

"Can Corey and I take one to my bedroom?" Ronnie asked. "I want to show him this book I found at the library."

"I'll carry it for you so you don't burn yourself," Lori said. A few minutes later, after setting the scented candle jar on top of Ronnie's tall dresser for safekeeping, she returned to the living room where she found Mac gathering the cups and bowls.

"You don't have to do that," she protested.

"Considering how dark it is in here, the chance of spills is rather high."

"Yes, but I'll get it." It unnerved her to have him perform such a domestic task for her when Glenn had refused to be bothered. He'd always left the household tasks, no matter how minor, to her. "You're in charge of the inside," he'd told her. Of course, the outside chores of mowing the lawn and taking out the trash had fallen into her domain as well, mainly because he'd simply been "too busy".

She stacked the cups and bowls, then carried her cargo to the kitchen counter with only a glimmer of light from the living room to guide her. As she turned to retrace her steps, she hit an immovable object.

"Whoa," Mac said as he gripped her arms to keep her from falling.

"I'm sorry," she said as her pulse raced in response to his touch. "I didn't realize you were behind me."

"I didn't think you did."

His hold lessened once she found her feet, but he didn't release her. A quiver of anticipation slid down her spine.

"Did you need something?" she asked, conscious of his breath mingling with hers.

"Yes, I do."

Before she could understand what he was talking about, he kissed her.

CHAPTER SIX

LATER, Lori would attribute her actions as a freak side effect of the storm, but at that moment it was as if the kisses she'd imagined had magically become reality.

Part of her mind tried to explain how this was an accident, a case of their heads being in the right place at the right time, but as the seconds passed and Mac's mouth never left hers, she gave up that argument.

He may not have purposely intended to kiss her, but he obviously didn't mind continuing.

Neither did she.

She melted against him and something in the dim recesses of her head noticed how he pulled her tightly against his body as if he were trying to mold her full length to his.

This feeling of finding her other half had been what she'd wanted, what she'd craved as long as she could remember.

Surely he noticed the electricity surging between them. Surely he noticed the connection that bound them on an emotional level. And surely he noticed that she held nothing back in the way she responded to his gentle assault on her senses.

The power clicked on without warning and what had been so magical, so *real*, suddenly couldn't stand up under the light. The mood disappeared with the darkness and frustration filled her at the poor timing. Mac released her—rather abruptly, she thought—and stepped back as a full range of emotions flashed across his face. An instant later, his professionally calm demeanor covered all of them.

She should say something—*anything*—but nothing came to mind.

"Lori," he began, his gaze riveted to hers, but Ronnie's voice from the other room interrupted.

"Mom, Mac," she called impatiently. "The TV's back on so we can watch the rest of the movie."

Lori turned, ready to join them, but Mac caught her arm. "Don't wait for us," he said loudly. "We'll catch up later."

They were obviously happy to comply because Lori didn't hear any objection.

"Lori," he said again. "I just want to say—"

"Please, don't," she said, shaking her head for emphasis as she distanced herself from him by several feet. "I already know what it is."

"Somehow, I don't think—"

"You're going to explain how it was a horrible mistake and how sorry you are. I can see it in your eyes."

"I'm not sorry."

She didn't believe him, no matter how sincere he looked. "You're not? Then what was that look of shocked horror all about?"

Mac ran one hand through his hair. "I'll admit I was surprised. I didn't expect the chemistry to be so..."

"Strong?"

"Yes. I didn't plan for this to happen, but you were there and the moment seemed right...Corey suggested that we get married."

"What?" The shift in conversation made Lori feel as if she'd missed something important.

"This afternoon, Corey suggested we get married."

"So that's what this was about? Your attempt to see if we were compatible?" She didn't know if she should be amused or angry, but the more she thought about it, the idea of punching him appealed to her. "Did I pass your test?"

"This wasn't a test. It was something that I wanted to do."

"Because Corey planted the idea?"

"No." He didn't hesitate. "I wanted to kiss you because you're a beautiful woman."

As confessions went, it made her feel slightly better. "And what do you want to happen next?"

"If you think about it..." He spoke tentatively. "Corey's suggestion makes perfect sense."

She stared at him, not bothering to hide her shock. "How?"

"We're practically a family now. You look after the kids after school, help them with their homework. We eat dinner together every night. That's more than a lot of households do, or so I hear. I'd love to have a daughter like Ronnie, and Corey thinks the world of you."

"I think he's a special kid, too, but marriage?" The suggestion was so unexpected, she could hardly take it in. Circumstances being what they were, she vacillated between being flattered and frightened. After rushing into her first marriage and living to regret it, she refused to repeat her mistake. This time she had Ronnie to consider, too, which forced her to be even more cautious.

"It would be a good decision for all of us," he told her. "Ronnie gets the father she wants, and neither of us will shoulder the burden of single parenting. We'll be a team."

His offer sounded good. *Too* good, in fact, and that scared her. Tying the knot with Glenn had been a practical decision, but she didn't want *practical*. She wanted a hot and heavy love affair. She'd clung to her dream for so long that she simply couldn't compromise or discard it so easily.

"If you're worried about the time I'd spend with you, then don't. Things will get better as soon as we hire another person or two."

He was right, but months could pass before that happened. "I don't deny that the children will benefit from having two parents, but my finances aren't in such dire straits that I need a wedding ring to take care of them. I'll take care of my debts whether I'm married or single." She studied him with curiosity. "You haven't said what you get out of this arrangement."

"Peace of mind. Companionship."

Someone to count on. He didn't say it, but she remembered it from a previous conversation. "What, exactly, do you mean by companionship?"

He met her gaze headon. "Someone to talk to, to share my day with. Considering that kiss, perhaps even a physical relationship. If you want to have one, that is."

Perhaps he could satisfy his natural urges without emotional entanglement, but she couldn't. "What about love?"

"Respect and mutual appreciation is just as important," he insisted. "Think of this as a business decision."

"Ah-h," she said slowly. "I get it. You can't find a housekeeper, so now you're willing to marry one. And if you get a bed partner, why, that's even better."

He frowned, clearly frustrated. "You're looking at this wrong."

She crossed her arms. "Then, please, straighten out my warped thinking."

"This is a win-win situation for everyone. We all get something we want."

"Except love."

Mac opened his mouth, then closed it with a snap.

She softened her tone. "I realize this is difficult for you to understand, but I want a marriage based on love and commitment, not one based on how much money is in your bank account or the fact that my daughter will have someone to take her to the next 'Donuts for Dads' breakfast."

"Commitment won't be a problem. I'll be faithful."

Elsa had been dead for eight years and he showed no signs of opening his heart to anyone else. Faithfulness was definitely one of Mac's strengths. On the other hand, if he was too loyal to let go, perhaps it *was* more of a flaw.

Yet if he'd said that he loved her, or had even *pretended*

along those lines, she would have said yes. Two weeks of getting to know him wasn't that long, but she knew all she needed to know—he was the most wonderful man she'd ever met and heaven forbid, she loved him.

She loved him. The revelation caught Lori by surprise and she wanted to shout out with joy, but she couldn't, just as she couldn't share that news with Mac.

Because he was still in love with his dead wife.

Until that small but significant fact changed enough for him to have room in his heart for her, too, any serious relationship between them was doomed before it began. A one-sided love wouldn't thrive, no matter what circumstances surrounded it.

She couldn't explain her real reasons, so she relied on the explanation she'd given him on another occasion. "I'm flattered you asked me, but I want a love that's capable of setting off fireworks between me and my husband. I missed out the first time around. I don't want to miss my chance again."

"Love can grow," he insisted. "As for fireworks, I don't think we have to worry about that. If one little kiss packs that much punch..."

Unfortunately, he didn't seem to understand that she wanted sparks borne out of love and not lust, but she let that thread drop. "What if it *doesn't* grow?"

"What guarantee do you have that you'll find your grand passion with the next guy you meet?" he countered.

"None," she said quietly, aware that for her no one could make her feel like Mac did. If he didn't love her, if he *wouldn't* love her, she wouldn't settle for anyone else, even if it meant she'd be alone for the rest of her life.

He paused. "We'd be good together."

"Oh, Mac," she wailed. "Don't make this harder than it already is."

"Then say yes."

"I can't," she said miserably, then added, "You aren't

going to let my decision affect Corey coming over here, are you?"

"No. Should I?"

"Of course not," she said impatiently. "Does he know that you were going to propose?"

Mac shook his head.

"Please, don't tell him," she begged. "He might think I've rejected him when I haven't."

"Of course not. You only rejected his father," he said wryly.

Lori couldn't stop herself from smoothing out the shirt wrinkle on Mac's chest. "I'm not rejecting you at all. I think we'd be good together, too, but a marriage should be based on the right reasons. Tell me something, though. Did you think I'd agree?"

"Honestly?"

"Honestly."

"No. I'd hoped you would, but..." He shrugged.

"No hard feelings?"

He stroked her chin. "None." A grin tugged at his mouth. "Maybe a few."

Ronnie and Corey appeared in the doorway. "The movie's over," Ronnie announced. "What can we eat?"

Mac didn't hesitate. "Pizza. My treat."

"That's not necessary," Lori protested. "I have meatloaf left from lunch."

At the two children's groans, Mac held up his hands. "It's three against one for pizza over meatloaf. You're outgunned, Mrs Ames, and outvoted."

The two youngsters ran into the other room, shouting with joy, while Mac hung back. "Something just occurred to me," he began. "If we handled my suggestion democratically, you'd be outvoted like you were on the pizza issue."

Although he acted as if he were delivering an offhanded remark, Lori understood the polite threat.

"You wouldn't call for a vote." If he did, she'd never have a moment's peace. "Would you?"

"I might."

"You're not playing fair."

"There are times to play fair and there are times when a person plays to win."

Unfortunately, she was the one with the most to lose.

The appearance of certain people spelled trouble, and Ruth Merriweather, St Anne's Risk Manager, fit in that category. Mac recognized that she was only doing her job in dealing with incidents of substandard care, but it would be nice if she'd occasionally share good news instead of bad.

He sipped his cup of coffee and scrawled his signature on the appropriate page in the chart before him. "What can I do for you today, Ruth?"

The fifty-year-old manager was five foot nothing and could barely see over the chest-high counter. As difficult as her job was on most days, she always wore a pleasant smile. "Can we talk?"

Mac leaned back in his chair. "What's on your mind?"

"I'd prefer it if we spoke privately."

That wasn't a good sign. "OK." He went to the glassed-in conference room at the center of the nurses' station where shift reports primarily took place. With the door closed, no one could hear their discussion, but if anyone needed him, they could see where he was. "What's up?"

Ruth opened her file and pulled out a familiar form. "I've gotten another incident report."

"On Brad Westmann?"

"How did you guess?" She was being facetious and they both knew it.

"What's he done now? Another charting error?"

"According to the report, he failed to adequately administer enough muscle relaxant to a patient who was undergoing a cystoscopy. Apparently, the patient reacted quite violently and the urologist now has to repair his bladder."

Mac winced. Although the kind of situation she'd described happened, anesthetists tried to avoid it at all costs. Surgeons didn't like their patients moving, especially not while they were inserting tubes or using sharp instruments.

"I'll talk to him."

"I've also received a report of an incident where he administered a drug containing sulfite to a patient with a known allergy."

Mac gritted his teeth. Sulfite was a common preservative added to a large number of drugs, and for the rare patient who was allergic to this chemical, alternatives had to be found.

"Fortunately, in this case, the patient only suffered a mild reaction. I don't need to tell you that we might not be so lucky next time."

"No, you don't."

"We've established quite a file on him. I realize that nurse-anesthetists are few and far between, and you haven't filled your last vacancy, but I'm afraid he's becoming a liability rather than an asset to the hospital."

"I'll deal with it."

"Good. Because, honestly, our attorneys get nervous when we see this sort of trend."

So do I. "I understand." The practice of anesthesia wasn't without risks, but minimizing them was the anesthetist's prime concern. Slipshod work couldn't be tolerated in this malpractice-happy climate. As much as he hated to do it, the time had come for more drastic measures than counseling and additional training sessions to solve the problem.

Making a mental note to meet with Brad as soon as they both had a free moment, Mac headed in the direction of his first patient.

"Good morning, Mr Collicott," he said to his eighty-year-old patient, who was scheduled for prostate surgery. "I'm here to talk to you about your anesthesia. Your questionnaire shows you're in good health."

Reed Collicott, whose graying hair had noticeably thinned, chortled. "I'm better than some folks my age, but if I was in fine shape, I wouldn't be here, sonny."

"I'll rephrase my comment. Other than your current problem, I see you're extremely healthy," Mac said with a smile. "You haven't had any history of heart disease, breathing problems like asthma or emphysema?"

"No troubles in those departments."

"Have you received anesthesia before?"

"Had surgery when I was in the Navy. I was at Pearl Harbor, you know."

"I didn't realize."

Reed grew pensive. "I remember that day just like it happened yesterday. Course, I don't expect anyone could forget a time like that. Anyway, I got hit and had some surgery on my legs."

"Did you experience any problems at the time?"

"None that I remember."

"How often do you drink alcohol?"

Reed chuckled. "Only on special occasions, although at my age every day is a special occasion."

Mac smiled. "How often?"

"I had a shot of whiskey last Christmas." He leaned closer. "If you promise not to tell my daughter, a friend and I always treat ourselves to a glass of wine every Saturday night. We think it's the reason we're both still able to kick up our heels, if you know what I mean."

Mac grinned. "I won't spill your secret. It's just the one glass?"

"Just one, sonny. Any more than that and we can't play pool. It requires a steady hand, you know."

"I know." Mac continued with his list of questions before he addressed the surgery itself. "For your procedure, we normally don't put you to sleep. A spinal block is usually adequate.''

Reed shook his head. "I don't mean to tell you your business, but I want to be knocked out before Dr Hanover starts, and I don't want to wake up until after he finishes."

"I can do that, but—"

"No buts. That's the way I want it."

"All right. Do you have any concerns? As you know, there are risks associated with any surgical procedure or drug we might give you."

"Aw, sonny, there's risks to crossing the street. If something happens, it happens. Life doesn't come with any guarantees. I'd rather go quick-like than suffer what those poor folks with Alzheimer's go through."

"Your chances of dying are very low."

"That's good. I've got a tournament to play just as soon as I heal up."

Mac suspected that Mr Collicott wasn't one to sit back and watch his golden years go by. Perhaps that was the secret to his good health and positive outlook.

His next patient, a four-year-old who was scheduled for a tonsillectomy, took more time. The mother grilled him over every little thing and required a lot of reassurance. Finally, he'd finished, but before he could take care of his next task, his pager beeped. The number on the display lifted his spirits.

"You rang?" he asked Lori as soon as he strode into the recovery room.

She looked worried as she pulled him aside to show him the chart on forty-two-year-old Erica Manning who'd just undergone a left radical mastectomy. "Her oxygen saturation has been dropping in spite of receiving oxygen. She complains of shortness of breath."

"Did you call for a blood gas?" Their treatment protocol included a standing order for an ABG once the oxygen saturation levels fell to a certain point.

"The report just came over the printer. Her paO2 is lower than it should be, but it hasn't reached the critical stage yet."

"Pneumothorax." While not every patient who underwent a mastectomy developed this complication, these people were more vulnerable than the patients who had lower abdominal surgeries.

She nodded, as if she'd suspected the diagnosis. "Do you want to insert a chest tube?"

"She's not in any real trouble at the moment. Let's get a quick chest X-ray and see what's going on. We might get by with just aspirating some of the air out of the pleural space."

"I'll get Radiology on the double."

"Where's the surgeon?"

"Dr Moss is in suite two. He's started a partial thyroidectomy and can't leave."

"OK. While you're arranging for the X-ray, I'll touch bases with him."

Thanks to the portable X-ray unit, Mac had the films in hand a short time later. Meanwhile, Lori never left her patient's side in case the woman's condition deteriorated rapidly.

"It looks as if only about fifteen per cent of her lung has collapsed," Mac told Lori. "Let's use a fourteen-gauge needle and syringe to aspirate the air. If that doesn't work and she gets worse, we'll insert a chest tube."

He explained the procedure to a semi-alert Mrs Manning while Lori set up a sterile field and laid out the supplies. Within seconds of Mac performing his procedure, Mrs Manning's labored breathing visibly eased.

"Let me know if she develops any more problems," he told Lori as he stripped off his gloves.

"I will."

"I see you're on tonight's call schedule."

"Yeah. I'm hoping it's quiet."

"Where will Ronnie go if you have to work?"

"Susannah is coming for a sleep-over."

"Are boys invited?"

She grinned. "It depends on how old the boy is."

"Is eight too old?"

"Are you on call, too?"

"I'm strictly back-up. So unless there's a massive highway wreck, I should have a quiet evening at home."

"If not, bring Corey by. I'll let Susannah know she might have another guest, just in case."

Mac arrived in suite two, gowned and ready for business, moments after a groggy Reed Collicott. Having received his pre-op medication, Reed was definitely relaxed.

"You won't forget what we talked about," he said as Mac sat on a stool behind his head.

"I won't forget," Mac assured him with a smile, although Reed couldn't see it behind his mask.

The urologist, Martin Hanover, arrived almost before Mac had finished speaking. At Martin's nod, Mac injected the dose of propofol into Reed's IV line. "In a few seconds, you'll be asleep," he told the man.

"Are you sure, sonny? I don't feel..." Reed's voice faded.

"Goodnight, sleep tight," Mac said. "OK, Martin. He's all yours."

"You're positive he's out?" Martin asked, clearly referring to the earlier incident involving Brad.

"Dead to the world," Mac replied.

Reed's surgery and the rest of the day passed uneventfully, although Mac's talk with Brad at the end of their shift didn't go well. Brad was defensive, which was only to be expected.

"I don't care about excuses," Mac told him. "These things can't happen. I don't want to be liable for errors that a person with your experience shouldn't be making. Neither does the hospital."

"Things are bound to happen. My caseload is heavy."

Mac felt a twinge of guilt for having a lighter month's schedule than usual. "I'm merely informing you that as of now you're back on probation. Another error and you'll be terminated."

Brad's face turned ruddy with anger. "You can't fire me."

"Yes, I can. Based on the volume of incidence reports we've collected, I wouldn't have any trouble showing the danger you pose to our patients. I'd be within my authority to release you from your contract. I'm hoping it won't come to that, but this is your final warning."

"Fine." Brad's entire body was stiff and Mac was glad he'd met with him at the end of the day rather than the beginning. It would be better for both staff and patients if Brad went home and cooled off. "Is that all?"

Wasn't it enough? "Yes," Mac answered. Alone, he exhaled deeply. The situation with Brad emphasized his need to get his household affairs in order so that he could deal with his responsibilities at work. The agency had exhausted its list of candidates, which meant that he had to choose among the ones he'd already interviewed if he didn't want to wait indefinitely. After the most recent reports concerning Brad, he simply couldn't cater to Corey's whims any longer. Not because he wouldn't like to, but because time had run out.

If only...

He headed for the parking lot and ran into Rob at the door.

"Rough day?" Rob commiserated.

"To put it mildly."

"How about dropping by the house for a beer? Gail's gone to a sorority meeting and Susannah's over at Lori's."

"I know."

"That's right. Lori's been watching Corey after school. How's it working out?"

"Corey's thrilled, but not having Martha has caused problems with my call schedule. I can't leave Corey at home when I go to work during the night. Finding a babysitter at two in the morning isn't an option and neither is dragging him to someone else's house."

"Have you had any luck finding a replacement?"

"We've narrowed it down to two applicants, but Corey isn't wild about either of them. I told him that he could choose, but I hadn't counted on it being so difficult to find the right person. With my staff situation as it is, I'm going to have to hire someone with or without Corey's approval."

"Too bad. He won't be happy."

"It can't be helped. The logical thing to do is marry Lori, but when I explained how it would be in everyone's best interests..."

Rob stopped in his tracks. "Back up a second. Did I hear you right?"

"It makes sense for both of us to combine forces," Mac said defensively. "Corey loves her, Ronnie wants a dad and—"

"Oho, buddy," Rob said. "You proposed by telling her how sensible it was?"

"What else could I do? I couldn't pledge undying love." Mac saw the shocked amusement on his friend's face. "I can't lie to her."

"Well, no, but..." he shook his head. "I can't believe you did that."

"I'll admit it was an impulsive act. If I'd thought things through, I might have couched it differently."

But what would he have said? Three little words—"I love you"—and only those three words would have gotten Lori to agree, but he refused to be like Glenn and tell her what she wanted to hear. He had more integrity than to stretch the truth, especially when it had a nasty habit of later slapping one in the face.

"Then she said no?"

"Didn't I say that?"

"Honestly, Mac, I don't claim to understand women but, after living with two of them, I've learned a few things. One of them is that they don't want logic. They want romance and they want to be swept off their feet."

"So I gathered," Mac said wryly. "Lori and I get along well enough and we have enough mutual attraction for romance." With the power unleashed from their one little kiss, passion wouldn't be a problem.

"I don't know," Rob said slowly. "I can't explain it, but with women romance isn't slam, bam, thank you, ma'am. Somehow their heads have to get involved. Their emotions."

"So what do I do? I tried to play on her emotions with how Corey needs her."

"She's not marrying Corey."

"No, but combining households makes such perfect sense." Sharing his house and his life with Lori would require some adjusting on his part, but he couldn't offer more than a mutually beneficial arrangement.

"You can't make sense out of affairs of the heart. It just doesn't work. So until you're ready to let someone love you and love them in return, you're going to have to make do with hired help. If you want my advice, though, you'll do whatever it takes to keep her."

Mac wanted to, but he didn't know if he could survive loving and losing someone again.

CHAPTER SEVEN

"You broke your promise," Corey accused, his small body shaking with fury as he stood in Mac's den.

Mac inhaled sharply. He'd known Corey would take the news badly, but he'd hoped to reason with him. "Now, son..."

"You said I could pick the housekeeper. You lied."

Mac left his desk to crouch beside his son. "I know, and I'm sorry. I wanted to find someone you liked, but I ran out of options. With problems at the hospital, I need to spend more time there."

"I don't like Mrs Partridge." He crossed his arms and turned his mouth into a pout. "I'd rather have Mrs Spillman."

Mac suspected as much, but he had absolutely no faith in her ability to run their household on an even keel, which was why he'd chosen Mrs Partridge. "You don't know her well enough to *not* like her," Mac said calmly. "Can't you give her a chance?"

"She's going to make me do homework all the time."

"I'll talk to her. I promise."

Corey's raised eyebrow revealed exactly what he thought of his father's promise.

A fresh wave of guilt stabbed Mac's chest. If the situation with Brad hadn't turned out as it had, and if he'd been able to find another anesthetist or two, things would be different. His grace period had simply come to an end sooner than he'd expected.

"Give her a chance," he repeated. "Please? If it doesn't work out, we'll make a new plan."

Corey's face remained settled in mutinous lines. "I still

106

don't understand why we need Mrs Partridge. I could stay with Lori on the nights you work.''

"I know you like spending time at their house. I do, too," Mac told him. "But this is your home."

"You won't be here, so why does it matter where I am?"

That barb stung. "I'm your father and I'm responsible for you," Mac said firmly. "We can't ask Lori to do this favor for us indefinitely. It was only a temporary measure."

"I want it to be permanent."

"I know you do," Mac soothed. He recalled Rob's advice. "Women need to feel special before they marry someone. They want dates, fancy dinners for two and flowers."

Corey's eyes widened. "Oh. We haven't done that, have we?"

Mac smiled. "No, we haven't." Convincing Lori of how good they would be together required time to do the very things he'd described—time he didn't have.

"Could you do that after Mrs Partridge comes?"

Mac hadn't thought of it before, but having a housekeeper could help in that regard. She could watch both children so he and Lori could enjoy a night out or at least a few hours alone. "It's possible."

"And I'd still get to visit Lori?"

"Of course." Mac frowned. "Did you think you wouldn't ever see her again? Is that why you don't like Mrs Partridge?"

Corey shrugged as he dug the toe of his shoe into the carpeting and avoided Mac's gaze. "Partly," he mumbled.

"Don't worry," Mac said as he hugged him, grateful to be able to dispel at least one of his son's fears. "We'll get together as often as possible."

For a moment Corey fell silent as he weighed the advantages and disadvantages. "I still don't like Mrs Partridge," he finally said. "And I'm still not happy because you didn't let me choose like you said I could."

"I know and I'm sorry."

"But I'll give her a try."

Corey's grudging acceptance was more than Mac had expected at the start of their conversation. "Thanks for giving her a chance. I'm proud of you for making that decision."

"But if she's mean..." Corey warned.

"I'll send her packing." He hoped the two of them got along. While he wouldn't hesitate to fire the woman, he was afraid of the damage it might inflict on his slowly growing relationship with his son. He'd never forgive himself if he lost the ground he'd gained.

"Dad hired a housekeeper," Corey informed Ronnie over the telephone.

"Then he doesn't want to marry my mom?"

"I'm not sure. He says he still loves my mom, but then he talked about taking Lori on dates and stuff like that. I guess he wants to get to know her better."

"Golly, Cor. If he doesn't know her by now..."

Corey knew Ronnie was just as disappointed as he was. "Yeah, but I'm not giving up yet."

"Do you think he'll marry Mrs Partridge instead?"

"Nah. She's too old. She's more like a grandma."

"A grandma would be nice."

"Not this one," Corey said darkly. "She doesn't smile much. Not like Martha."

Her voice brightened. "Maybe your dad will miss coming to our house. We always had a good time at dinner."

A ray of hope pierced his gloom. "Do you think so?"

"He has to," she said fiercely. "I miss you and you're not even gone yet."

Corey agreed. He didn't want to go back to eating dinner in silence and seeing his dad only before school every morning.

"Maybe you should call your aunt Liz and ask her what

to do," Ronnie suggested. "She could even talk to your dad for you."

"I'll email her," Corey said. Surely his aunt could convince his dad to marry Lori.

Ronnie stared at the bowl in front of her. "This is moo goo what?"

"Moo goo gai pan," Lori informed her daughter. "Try it. It's delicious."

Ronnie looked at Corey who nodded his encouragement. "OK," she said. "If Corey likes it, I'll taste it."

Carefully hiding her smile from her daughter, Lori exchanged an amused glance with Mac before she placed a spoonful on top of Ronnie's rice.

It was Friday evening, the end of the first week of their final two weeks together and the time had passed faster than Lori would have liked. Mac had worked late every night, usually arriving near Corey's bedtime. Tonight, however, he'd ended his day on time and had served dinner at his house, courtesy of The Chinese Garden.

"What do you think?" Lori asked Ronnie as she tentatively tasted the bean sprouts.

She looked thoughtful before she spoke. "I like it. Can I have my fortune cookie now?"

"Finish your egg roll first," Mac told her. "In the meantime, I want to hear about your day at school."

Lori listened while both children shared bits and pieces about their teacher and classmates. She'd heard it all earlier, but she didn't mind listening again. She'd missed having Mac around for dinner and she savored every detail, memorizing them to recall at a later date.

"We're done," Corey announced as soon as they'd cracked open their cookies and read the fortunes inside. "May we be excused?"

"Yes, you may," Lori answered.

The two shot away from the table and headed for Corey's

room. Lori studied Mac from across the oak table capable of seating twelve. "You look exhausted," she commented, noticing the lines of strain around his mouth and eyes.

"It's been a rough week."

"How long will you be overseeing Brad?" Word had leaked out that the nurse-anesthetist was on probation. He no longer handled cases alone, which meant that either Mac or Josh, the other anesthesiologist, had to watch him perform his duties or assume them altogether. Of course, this was on top of Mac's usual workload and responsibilities.

Mac rubbed his eyes. "I'm not sure. Josh and I will reevaluate the situation in a month. On a more encouraging note, we have a lead on an applicant."

"I'm glad to hear it. Out of curiosity, who's on call this weekend since it was Brad's turn?"

"I am," he said ruefully. "Everyone else had plans that couldn't be changed."

His voice sounded as tired as he looked. "Why don't you go into the living room and relax?" she suggested. "I'll clean this up and—"

He shook his head. "I didn't invite you here to work. This was supposed to be your night off, remember?"

"Yes, but—"

"I'm serious."

She rose. "I am, too. If you think I'm going to sit and watch you work when you're dead on your feet, you can think again. By the way, Corey mentioned that he's out of clean clothes."

Mac pinched the bridge of his nose. "Yeah, he said something about it this morning. I'd better toss a load into the washing machine."

"Do that," Lori ordered. "I'll take care of this and we'll finish at the same time."

He hesitated. "Are you sure?"

"Yes. On our next visit, I'll sit back and act like a lady

of leisure, but for now, I'll appreciate your good intentions.'' She smiled.

He grinned. "Fair enough."

As she'd predicted, by the time Mac returned from the laundry room, she'd stored the leftovers in the refrigerator in their cardboard cartons and had stacked the dishes in the dishwasher.

"If I'd been thinking, I would have asked Susannah to babysit while we went to the movies," he said as he led the way to his living room.

"You wouldn't have had any luck. It's football night and the high school team plays at home. I'm sure we'll find something on television to watch."

"Everyone at work was talking about a Discovery Channel documentary about sunken ships. How does that sound?"

She didn't care as long as she could spend a few hours with him. "Sunken ships is fine with me," she said cheerfully as she sat beside him on his sofa with his arm around her.

Fifteen minutes into the program, she noticed Mac's breathing had changed. He'd fallen asleep.

Ten minutes later, Corey came running in. "Dad," he shouted. "Dad!"

Lori answered, hating to see Mac's rest interrupted. "He's sleeping. What's wrong?"

"The washer is making thumping noises," he said.

"I'll fix it." She eased her way out of Mac's loose embrace. He was obviously out for the count if Corey's shrill voice hadn't disturbed him.

Lori adjusted the clothes and the machine finished its spin cycle quietly. While she waited to throw the load in the dryer, she folded a load of towels, noticing the spots of bleached-out color spattered across them.

Poor Mac. He definitely needed a housekeeper.

Or a wife.

She tossed Corey's clothes into the dryer and returned to the living room where Mac hadn't moved a muscle. It was tempting to snuggle in beside him, to rest her head on his shoulder, to hold him close, but she didn't. When she did those things, she wanted Mac fully awake.

A fleece blanket hung over the back of an easy chair and she covered him with it before she settled down to watch the rest of the program.

When the credits rolled, he sat up. "I fell asleep," he said, sounding incredulous. "I didn't mean to."

"It's OK. You were tired. And speaking of tired, I need to get Ronnie to bed, too."

He rubbed his face and she heard the rasp of his stubble against his fingertips. "This wasn't how I thought the evening would go."

She chuckled. "There will be others." She hoped.

"Count on it," he said.

A week later, Lori finished stirring the pot of home-made spaghetti sauce she'd made at Corey's request and faced the two youngsters. "I know this is our last night before Mrs Partridge moves in, but I want you to know that every Friday is for us."

Corey nodded. "I won't forget."

"And you can come over on any other day after school or on the weekends," she said as she gave the little boy a hug and swallowed the lump in her throat. She hated good-byes and although she'd see Corey occasionally, it would be different. "Our door is always open."

He nodded, but his red-rimmed eyes gave away his relief.

"Come on, Corey," Ronnie suggested. "Let's go play while Mom gets dinner ready."

Lori returned to her meal preparations. Mac had promised he wouldn't be late on their last official evening together. Now, with thoughts of the Grant men's paths diverging from hers, she hated the idea.

Marry Mac.

She was so very tempted but, loving him as she did, she didn't think she could share him with a ghost. If she was meant to be Mac's wife, it would happen, whether it was now or later. After proving the truth in the adage "Marry in haste, repent in leisure" with her first marriage, she was wise to be cautious the second time around.

"Something smells good." Mac entered the kitchen, interrupting her thoughts.

"You're early," she said, surprised to see him.

He glanced at the clock. "I guess so. Shall I come back later?"

"Don't be silly. The pasta is going in the water even as we speak," she said, putting action to her words.

Mac lifted the lid on the pot of sauce. "Corey's favorite."

"Of course. I even baked a cake in his honor."

"Your four-layer fancy creation?" he teased.

"Complete with raspberries and frosting roses."

"You're giving him quite a send-off."

"He's a special boy. Anyway, I thought it might ease his transition. He's worried about your new housekeeper."

"I know. I thought he was used to the idea, but the closer we've gotten to the day, the less he's said to me."

"He's anxious and frightened. Life as he knows it will change again. It's bound to make anyone uptight."

"I suppose. I just wish he understood that I didn't have a choice."

Lori placed a hand on his arm. "He does, but it's tough for an eight-year-old to accept. He's lived through a lot of changes and he probably feels as if he's lost in the shuffle."

"How?"

"From his point of view, he's been passed from one caretaker to another. I'm not criticizing, mind you," she hurried to add. "I'm just telling you how he feels."

"He actually said this?"

"More or less. You're in an impossible situation, Mac. I'm only mentioning it so you know to make amends in other ways. Take him to the park or go to the movies. Don't ignore him."

"I'll try, but you've seen how the past two weeks have been. The next few won't be any easier."

"Try. By the way, I've told Corey that he has a standing Friday night date with us."

He grinned. "Does your invitation include parents?"

"Of course." Satisfied that she'd done all she could for Corey, she changed the subject. "I think the spaghetti is cooked. Would you call everyone to dinner?"

Lori kept the mood light as they ate and she avoided all references to Mrs Partridge. Corey's eyes glowed when she served dessert.

"Is this the somersault cake?" he asked. "The one you make just for special occasions?"

"The exact one. And you can take the leftovers home with you."

"Gee, Dad. Isn't that great?" he said, apparently forgetting that he wasn't too happy with his father.

"It certainly is."

Lori winked at Ronnie who slipped away from the table and returned with a package wrapped in airplane paper.

Corey's eyes couldn't have grown any larger. "For me?" he asked.

"You bet."

"Can I open it now?"

"Now's as good a time as any."

He ripped the wrapping and once he'd removed the lid he oohed over the contents. "Wow."

Lori smiled at his obvious delight. "It's a care package for you. I hope you'll enjoy it."

"I will." He lifted out a pack of Old Maid cards, several "Arthur" books and a Magic Schoolbus story that were duplicates of ones Ronnie owned and Corey liked, a box of Tinker Toys, a pad of writing paper and a pack of colored pens.

"We thought that you and your dad could play some of

your favorite games at home. And when we come over to visit, we can play, too."

It was nearly ten o'clock when Corey and Ronnie started yawning, bringing an official end to the evening. "Thanks for staying so late," she told Mac as she gathered Corey's things.

"I didn't have the heart to make him leave before he was ready. I appreciate you making this night special."

"It was my pleasure. I think it helps for him to know that he'll be back next Friday. He can hold onto that thought all week long."

"I'm sure he will. Mrs Partridge moves in tomorrow, so we're going to have a busy weekend."

"If you need anything, please, let me know."

"I will." While Mac loaded the car with Corey's presents and the leftover cake, Lori hugged Corey. "OK, big guy. Do you remember my phone number?" At his nod, she said, "I'm expecting you to call me every night at eight and tell me how your day went. Can you do that?"

"I won't forget."

She hugged him again, soaking in the feel of his little body. How he'd wriggled into her heart so quickly amazed her, but he had and now she felt as if he was taking a piece of her with him. Which was silly, of course. He was only about ten blocks and a phone call away. "I love you, Corey."

"I love you, too."

Deep in her own misery caused by a sudden attack of self-doubt, she couldn't watch them drive away. Instead, she closed the door and hugged Ronnie, who clearly shared her unhappiness. As she tidied the house before going to bed, Lori hoped that Mac wouldn't forget to carve out time for his son.

The following Wednesday, Blythe cornered Mac outside the nurses' station where he was on his way to another patient's pre-op visit. "Do you have a minute, Dr Grant?"

"Sure. What can I do for you?"

"What are the odds of getting a bad batch of morphine?"

"Slim to none. What's wrong?"

She dug a vial out of her pocket. "Lori brought this to my attention. She's given a dose out of this vial, but the patient doesn't respond to the painkiller. It's like it's lost its strength or something."

Mac glanced at the vial and the remaining contents. The liquid was colorless and clear, which didn't mean anything in terms of its efficacy since that was its normal appearance.

"You're sure?"

"It involved one of my patients, so she called me. I didn't know what to do, except try an unopened vial. It was fine and the patient experienced almost immediate relief."

"This is unusual," Mac agreed. "Is this the first time it's happened?"

"As far as I know, but you might ask Lori."

"If it's just the one vial, I suppose it's possible, but..." He shook his head. "It's just not likely."

"That's what I thought, which is why I brought it to your attention. Someone else might run into the same thing, so we should be alert."

Mac studied the label. "Had this vial been opened prior to this dose?"

"I believe so, but I don't know for which patient."

He didn't know what to think, but something definitely wasn't right. "Thanks. I'll keep my ears open in case anyone else reports a problem."

Puzzled by Blythe's report, he mentioned the situation to Josh when he caught up to him.

"I can't explain it," Josh said.

Determined to track down an answer, Mac went to the chemistry laboratory where he spoke to the technologist on duty. "Can you test the fluid and see what concentration of morphine is in this vial?"

The tech shook his head. "I can give you a qualitative

result, but not a quantitative answer. Our drug testing only detects a particular substance's presence. It won't tell how much is present."

"That'll have to do." He allowed the fellow to remove a small sample of the fluid, but kept the vial. Why, he wasn't sure, but he felt compelled to keep the evidence himself.

"Do you want me to call with the results?"

"I'd appreciate it," Mac said.

An hour later, he received his answer.

"I don't know what this fluid is," the tech told him, "but there's barely enough morphine present to give a trace result. Whoever is getting that for their pain isn't getting their money's worth."

"Thanks," Mac said. The mystery had grown and now he contacted the pharmacy.

"We haven't had anything like this happen before," the chief pharmacist said. "The vials from that lot have been distributed all over the hospital and yours is the first I've heard of with a problem."

"It's probably an isolated incident," Mac decided. "We're going to be extra conscientious, so if we see it happen again, we may need to pull all those meds off the shelves."

This was just what Mac needed—something else to demand his attention. His sleuthing had disrupted his schedule and now it looked as if he'd be working on into the evening. What made it worse was that he'd promised to play cards with Corey before bedtime.

At least Mrs Partridge had taken his household in hand and had whipped it back into shape. No more worrying about arriving at Lori's too late; no more feeling as if he were taking advantage of her; and no more concerns about dragging Corey out at night. His house sparkled, he found clean clothes in his closet, and if the meals weren't as tasty as Lori's because of his housekeeper's dietary restrictions, it seemed a small price to pay to have his routine back.

Sadly, his routine now seemed so...routine. He missed those evenings he'd grown to enjoy. He especially missed seeing Lori with her hair hanging loosely over her shoulders, her faded blue jeans molded to her slim curves and her smile that turned a bad day into a good one. For years he hadn't been concerned if his professional life had overshadowed his personal one, but in the space of a few weeks he realized how much he wanted to juggle the two successfully.

He needed someone to help him, and if he couldn't have Lori, then Mrs Partridge was the next best thing. He'd been so busy that he hadn't seen Corey since Sunday except in passing. Guilt over how he'd all but dumped him into her care niggled at him, but Corey hadn't complained about the woman so Mac guessed they were managing.

He wished that he could say the same for his problems at work.

On Thursday, Lori cornered him early in the morning. "At the risk of making you angry when you hear what I have to say," she said without preamble, "I'm going to say it anyway. I'm worried about Corey."

"Oh? He didn't complain about anything this morning."

"Of course not. He *can't. That woman* won't let him say anything to you."

"Now, Lori. Mrs Partridge assures me they're getting along perfectly."

She narrowed her eyes. "What does Corey tell you?"

"I've gotten home late every night, so we haven't talked."

"My point exactly. Do you realize that she won't let him call me at eight before he goes to bed?"

"Are you sure?" He couldn't imagine why she'd restrict Corey's daily phone call to Lori.

"Of course I'm sure." Lori stood toe to toe with him as she poked him in the chest. "He can't call because she makes him turn in at seven."

"It is early, I'll admit, but—"

"But nothing. Did you know that she also put him on a schedule this week? According to Ronnie, he gets fifteen minutes to eat his snack after school, thirty minutes to play outside, an hour for homework and another hour for extra reading. Plus, she only allows him fifteen minutes to use the internet and he can only access it if she's in the room. How would you feel if someone treated you like that?"

He inwardly winced. "She's obviously a little obsessive."

"A little? A little?" she screeched. "She's Attila the Hun. My gosh, Mac, Corey is a little boy and he needs time to play and relax without someone staring over his shoulder."

He rubbed his head. "All right. I'll talk to her. I know he's not fond of her, but are you sure he's not stretching the truth a little?"

"I spoke with her myself to remind her that Corey would be coming home with me tomorrow after school and she acted as if I was going to corrupt him. And don't say I'm imagining things, because I'm not," she warned. "One week together isn't very long but, believe me, he's not happy."

"OK. I'll talk to Mrs Partridge."

"Good." Her shoulders heaved with a cleansing breath. "I know you're busy, but you need to ease Corey into this transition."

"I'm doing the best I can, but I can't be in two places at once."

"Then you'd better decide which one is more important. You're not the only anesthesiologist on staff, but you are Corey's only parent."

With that, she stomped out of the recovery room, leaving him to feel like an errant schoolboy. He was caught in a tug of war and he simply didn't know what direction to turn. What sort of father was he if he didn't even know the depths of his son's distress?

He'd always taken Corey to school each morning, even

while Martha had been with them, but Monday had been rather hectic at their house and he'd gratefully turned over the task when Mrs Partridge had volunteered. To his shame and regret, he hadn't taken it back.

As for going to bed early, she had always informed him that Corey was tired. Never once had she mentioned the schedule she'd put in place.

It was a sad commentary on his own abilities to read people if Corey had seen this coming but he hadn't. He'd even promised him that he'd talk to her about this very subject, and now Corey would tally another broken vow to Mac's credit.

He hunted for Lori and found her in the lounge. "I'm going to call Corey after school."

Two red spots burned in her cheeks as she avoided his gaze, giving the impression that she was still too angry to look at him. "He'll appreciate it."

"This has been a tough week for all of us." God help him, he wanted her to understand that he hadn't planned things to happen as they had. Her opinion mattered, although he wasn't quite sure why. It just did.

She crossed her arms as if totally unconvinced by his defense. "It's been the hardest on Corey."

"I know. I'm trying."

She raised one eyebrow. "Are you?"

"Yes, dammit, I am." He hadn't meant to raise his voice, but he did.

To her credit, she didn't cower. "I'm not the person you have to convince. Corey is."

Having said her piece, Lori planned to walk away, but couldn't. "Look," she began in a more reasonable tone, "I know you're doing your best. I know you're short-staffed and you have the morphine issue to worry about, too." She hoped it was an isolated incident caused by a manufacturing error, but it could easily be something far more insidious. Drug abuse among members of the anesthesiology profession wasn't uncommon, thanks to the inherent availability of the various medications and the stresses of the job. "Please, don't lose Corey in the shuffle."

Mac nodded, but didn't answer.

She returned to the PACU, emotionally drained from worry and her confrontation. Perhaps she'd overreacted and been overly harsh, but part of her anger was directed at herself. If she hadn't stubbornly clung to her fairy-tale notion of love, Corey wouldn't have been placed in an intolerable situation.

On the other hand, if she'd married Mac, he'd let her fill the gaps in Corey's life just as easily as he'd allowed Mrs Partridge to fill them. In the end, the poor child would never know his father except as the man who occasionally visited his own home. It would be like seeing Glenn's awkward relationship with Ronnie all over again.

She was damned if she did, and damned if she didn't.

At school, instead of waiting for Ronnie to run to the car, Lori went into the school. She wanted to see Corey and talk to him herself but, according to Ronnie, he'd left early for a dentist appointment.

Tomorrow, she promised herself. Tomorrow was Friday and their planned get-together. Although she wanted to wade into the fray and straighten the situation out right now, she had to give Mac time to take care of it himself.

"How was your dentist appointment?" Mac asked Corey. "Any cavities?"

"No. When are you coming home?"

Mac glanced at his watch. Five-thirty. "In a couple of hours."

"Things aren't working out, Dad. Nothing is going like I thought it would. We haven't taken Lori on a date or invited her over for dinner."

"I know. I've been really busy—" Mac began.

Corey continued as if he hadn't spoken. "And *she*—" his emphasis leaving no doubt as to who *she* was "—said if I don't get a hundred on my spelling test tomorrow, I can't go home with Lori for our Friday night date." His voice rose. "It's not supposed to be this way. You promised."

Guilt struck Mac hard. "Calm down, son. It's OK."

"No, it's not. It's *horrible*. You don't know because you're not here."

Mac rubbed the back of his neck as he spoke into the receiver. "I'll be home by seven. Seven-thirty at the latest. We'll hash this out then."

"OK, but I won't go to bed," Corey warned. "Even if she makes me."

"You won't have to," Mac told him. "I'll see you shortly."

With his son appeased, he replaced the receiver and wondered what tasks he could postpone until tomorrow.

A light sleeper, Lori woke at one a.m., startled by what she thought was a knock at the door. Don't be ridiculous, she thought. Who would come over at this time of night?

She heard the sound again. It *was* a knock, she decided before she threw on her robe and hurried through the house.

To her surprise, she saw Mac standing on the porch, his coat collar turned up against the cold air.

Fear instantly gripped her chest and she flung open the door. "What's wrong?"

"Is Corey here?"

The sickening feeling grew. "Why no. Isn't he at home?"

Mac shook his head and worry lines bracketed his mouth. "I've looked everywhere. He's missing."

CHAPTER EIGHT

"Missing?" Lori's stomach twisted into a giant knot. "Since when?"

Mac ran one hand through his hair. "Sometime after ten, I think. I peeked in on him when I got home and he was asleep."

"Then how did you know he'd left?"

"I worked in my office until midnight when I checked on Corey one last time. He breathes with a funny little snuffle when he's asleep and when I couldn't hear it from the doorway, I went to his bed. He'd arranged his pillows and covers so it would look like he was lying there when he wasn't." He turned worried eyes in her direction. "He ran away."

Too stunned to stand, Lori sank onto the sofa. "Something must have happened this evening. He wouldn't just leave, not when he knew we were expecting him tomorrow night. Today," she corrected herself.

"Several things happened," Mac said flatly. "First, he's upset with me. I'd promised to be home by seven so we could meet with Mrs Partridge and talk about her rules. A car wreck and three emergency surgeries ruined that idea. Anyway, as soon as I realized he was gone, I roused Mrs Partridge. She admitted how furious Corey had been after she threw out the cake you'd made."

"Why did she do that?"

"She said he ate too much sugar." Lori sputtered her dismay as Mac continued, "Apparently Corey was so angry he dumped his dinner in the trash. She immediately sent him to his room for punishment."

Now the youngster's actions made sense. "And when

you didn't come home on time, he decided that he couldn't, or wouldn't, take any more."

"I'd say you're right."

"Why, that...that...*woman*. How could she have been a schoolteacher and be so insensitive?"

"I don't know, but she's packing her bags as we speak. I would have called, but I was afraid I'd do something I'd regret later if I stayed, so I left."

Lori's vision blurred. "Oh, Mac, I feel as if I'm to blame." Her cake had been the final straw for Corey and her decision had brought Mrs Partridge into their life.

"It's not your fault," he said, sounding defeated. "It's mine. I relied on a person who wasn't reliable. I'm the one who is ultimately responsible."

"We can sort that out later," Lori said, pulling herself together for Mac's sake. "Let's find him first."

"Which is why I'm here," he said. "Do you have any idea where he might have gone?"

Lori shook her head. "Not a one."

"Has Ronnie said anything?"

"Not to me."

"I can't believe he's gone, Lori. I don't know what I'll do if..."

His voice died and she rose to hug him. He felt warm and solid and she found it very comforting. "We will," she said fiercely. "Have you called the police?"

"Not yet. I was hoping he'd be here with you."

It was time for action, even if it was one a.m. "I'll call Rob and Gail. They'll watch Ronnie while I help you look for Corey."

He paced while she placed the call and explained. A few minutes later, with Gail's promise that they would be right over echoing in her ears, she hurried into her bedroom to change into a pair of jeans and a white sweatshirt. Aware of how tangled her hair was, she dashed into the bathroom, tied it at the back of her neck and rinsed the sleep out of her eyes before rejoining Mac in the living room.

Ronnie stumbled down the hall behind her. "What's going on, Momma?" she asked as she yawned.

"Corey's missing," Lori said gently. "Do you know where he might be?"

Instantly, she came alert. "No." A moment of indecision suddenly flitted across her face and Mac crouched beside her.

"If you know where he is, you have to tell us," he said gently. "It's cold outside and I'm worried about him."

"That's just it," Ronnie said, her eyes huge. "I don't know. At least, not for sure."

"Where do you *think* he might be?" Lori coaxed.

"He's talked a lot about his aunt Liz. He said that he wanted to stay with her."

"Liz." Mac snapped his fingers. "I never thought of her."

"Does she live near us?"

"Several hundred miles west," he said dryly.

Lori turned back to her daughter. "Did he say how he was going to get there?"

Ronnie shook her head. "You're going to find him, aren't you?"

"Yes, we are." Mac sounded determined.

His resolve was comforting, but Lori's fear still coalesced into a knot in her throat. There were far greater dangers than the weather to an eight-year-old boy trying to travel alone—dangers too horrible to be considered. Certain people preyed upon innocent youngsters and if he fell into the wrong hands...

"Surely he wouldn't try to hitchhike," she said, trying not to let her imagination run wild. "Would he?"

Mac visibly shuddered as if he'd imagined the same grisly scenario that she had. "Who knows? He's upset so it's hard to say what decision he'll make. In the meantime, I'll call my sister."

While he was punching in the number on his cellphone, Rob and Gail arrived, looking as worried as Lori felt. She quietly explained the situation as she watched Mac pace the floor like a caged tiger. Lori could see how this development had shattered him. For all of his faults, for all of his dedication to his job and his patients, and in spite of his difficulty in sharing himself with his son, he did love him.

"All right, sweet pea," she told Ronnie. "You need to go back to bed. Rob and Gail will stay until I get back."

"You're going to find him, aren't you?" Ronnie repeated.

"We won't rest until we do," Lori promised as she led her to her room and snapped on the lights.

Ronnie scrambled under the duvet. "Why can't we be a family, Mommy? Corey wouldn't have had that mean old Mrs Partridge telling him what to do and he wouldn't have run away."

Lori tried not to give ground to the guilt that had wrapped itself around her heart and refused to let go. Her idea to hold out until Mac loved her wasn't supposed to turn out like this. Her selfish wish had caused a little boy untold mental anguish and may have cost him his life.

Unable to deal with her daughter's question, she simply repeated the phrase that had become her mantra. "We'll find him. Now, go to sleep. Rob and Gail are here if you need anything."

She kissed Ronnie's forehead, hugged her, then switched off the lights. Eager to begin the search—failure wasn't an option—she returned to the living room where the Naylors and a stone-faced Mac waited.

"Well?" Lori demanded. "Did you talk to your sister?"
Did he talk to his sister?
Mac had barely gotten a word in edgewise once she'd

recognized his voice. His ears still rang from the blistering Liz had given him. According to her, she'd called both his home and the hospital as soon as she'd read Corey's email, but she'd never gotten through and obviously no one had passed along her messages. He thought of the stack on his desk at the hospital and winced. So much of this could have been avoided if he wasn't torn in fifteen different directions, but recriminations would have to wait until he found Corey, safe and sound.

"Liz received an email from Corey yesterday," he began. "He mentioned how upset he was about the housekeeper. How he wanted to..." His throat closed as he tried to say that Corey had wanted to live with her instead of him. Corey's rejection cut more deeply than Mac had ever dreamed possible. Instead, he simply said, "He told her what he'd told Ronnie."

The compassion in Lori's eyes as she understood his meaning and his pain nearly undid him. He would have deserved any scolding she gave him but, rather than lash out, she held her tongue and squeezed his hand in silent support.

"Why don't we go back to your house and call the police from there?" she said quietly. "If we're lucky, Corey may have calmed down and come home."

Mac nodded, although in his heart he knew otherwise. Corey had made up his mind, planned his actions, and nothing, short of a miracle, would change things.

Mac wanted a miracle.

By the time Mac returned to his house with Lori in tow, Mrs Partridge had wiped out all traces of her presence. From the way Lori marched into the house, if the housekeeper had been there, Mac thought it highly likely that she would have either left on a stretcher or, at the very least, with a black eye.

By the time the police arrived, Mac had searched Corey's room with Lori's help. As he reviewed the history on his son's computer, Mac wasn't sure if he was relieved to discover that Corey hadn't made any travel plans over the internet. He'd heard of kids purchasing airline tickets online, but Corey obviously hadn't done so.

Where was he?

The policeman wasn't much help. "If he's already left town, it may take some time before we have a lead," Officer Tracey warned. "The truck stop at the edge of town is always busy, day or night. Whoever might have seen him may be long gone."

"But you will ask around?" Mac said.

"Yes, we will." Armed with Mac's cellphone number and his description of an eight-year-old boy wearing a red baseball cap, a navy blue insulated winter coat and jeans, and carrying a black backpack, the officer returned to his squad car.

"And now we wait," Lori said. "Would you like some coffee?"

"Sure. Whatever you want." Hearing the words come from his own mouth reminded him of how Corey said the same things whenever he was resigned to his fate. God, how he missed him already.

Deep in his thoughts, Mac didn't notice Lori had disappeared until she pressed a mug into his hands.

"I don't want to lose him, Lori," he said.

She began kneading his shoulders and although he appreciated her effort, he couldn't possibly relax until Corey returned. "I know you don't," she said. "You won't."

"He wants to live with Liz."

"I'm sure he doesn't mean it. He's angry and upset and he thinks it's his only option to get out of a bad situation."

Mac sipped the coffee, focusing on the pain of the hot liquid against his tongue instead of the pain in his heart.

He stood abruptly. "I can't sit here and do nothing."

"All right," she said. "Where do you want to go?"

"I don't know. Anywhere but here."

Within minutes, Mac was driving through the quiet streets. "Do you think he might have gone to one of his friends' houses?"

"It's possible," Lori said, "but he never talked of one in particular."

"Where did he like to go when he was with you?"

"We didn't visit too many places," Lori admitted. "Other than the library, the grocery or video stores were our usual haunts. If he intends to reach your sister's, though, he won't waste time walking through town."

"Let's hope someone at the truck stop saw him," he said fervently. He'd barely survived after Elsa's death. If anything happened to Corey, Mac would never be able to live with his guilt. Not in a million years.

He drove past the high school and immediately Lori grabbed his arm. "Look! The bus barn."

Mac glanced at the huge building that housed all the district's school buses. "Yeah, so?"

"Corey loves the Magic Schoolbus books."

"Is that significant?" He couldn't understand why she was getting excited over a schoolbus.

"Yes, it is." She nearly bounced in her seat. "If you haven't read those books, they're about kids who go with their teacher on all sorts of wonderful, magical trips. They visit places under the sea, inside the body, into space—that sort of thing."

"OK."

"What I'm saying is," she explained, "the bus takes them places. Now, he knows the school bus isn't going to take him to his aunt's, but if he's done his homework, and I suspect he has, he's learned about our bus service."

Mac finally understood. "Then he may be at the station."

"Isn't it worth a drive over there to check it out?"

Immediately, Mac rounded the corner and headed in the opposite direction. "Do you know their schedule?"

"I wish I did," Lori remarked fervently. "If he's there, I hope he's OK. The bus depot isn't in a very good part of town."

Mac remembered more than one Saturday night when they'd patched up stabbing victims in the OR. The thought of Corey being in that environment turned his foot on the gas pedal to lead.

He arrived in less than five minutes when it should have taken twice as long. The parking lot was empty, the interior still dark. Clearly, the company wasn't open for business.

"He's not here," he said flatly.

Lori leaned forward to peer through the windshield. "It's cold. He may have crawled behind those bushes near the entrance to wait."

Mac didn't wait for further instructions. He drove onto the sidewalk and parked so that his headlights illuminated the front of the building. Before he'd rolled to a complete stop, Lori jumped out of her side. Mac slammed the gear into "Park", but didn't shut off the engine in his rush to follow.

"Mac, look."

He saw the bundle of clothing wedged between the brick building and the evergreen, and his heart seemed to flip-flop in his chest. He knelt down and recognized the red baseball cap through his suddenly blurred vision.

He'd been given a second chance. He didn't deserve it, but fate had been kind. He wouldn't let this miracle go to waste, no matter what he might have to do.

His hand trembled as he touched Corey's coat. For a long moment, he simply drank in the sight of his sleeping child as he breathed silent thanks over and over again.

"Is he OK?" Lori peered over his shoulder.

"I think so." Not wanting to scare him, he called his name. "Corey. Corey, it's me. Time to wake up."

Corey raised his head, his face streaked with dirt and

dried tears. "Dad?" he asked, blinking owlishly in the glare of the headlights. "Lori?"

Mac cleared his throat. "Yeah, son. We're here. We've been looking for you for hours."

"I'm going to Aunt Liz's," he said defiantly.

"That's what she told me when I called her," Mac said. "Before you go, maybe we should talk."

"I don't know about you," Lori said as her teeth began chattering, "but I'm cold. Would you mind if we talked about your trip in your dad's car where it's warm?"

Mac had wondered how they'd win Corey's co-operation, but Lori had obtained it with ease. Corey crawled out from behind the bush, dragging his backpack. As soon as he was free, Mac couldn't contain himself. He hugged him until Corey protested.

"Dad, you're squeezing the stuffing out of me."

"I can't help it." Mac loosened his hold. "I was so worried about you. So was Lori."

"I was fine, Dad."

Mac opened his mouth to argue, but Lori forestalled him with a hand on his arm and a small frown. "My toes are frozen," she announced cheerfully, although Mac knew that fifty-degree weather wouldn't have affected her as quickly as she'd claimed.

"Then let's get warm," Mac said.

A few minutes later he'd installed Corey in the back seat of his car, where Lori also chose to sit. "Much better," she said in her familiar lilt as she tucked him under her arm.

"Am I in trouble?" Corey asked.

Mac twisted his body to reassure himself that they'd actually found him. Worry made his voice sound harsh, although he didn't intend to sound angry. "What do you think?"

"If you want my opinion," Lori inserted cheerfully, "I

think we need a cup of hot chocolate before we get into a big discussion. Would you like to go to my house?"

Corey nodded.

"Home, James," Lori teased, as if Mac were the chauffeur.

A small smile tugged on Corey's mouth, and for that Mac would have driven him anywhere. "OK. Lori's house it is."

As he drove off, he dialed the police station on his cellphone and alerted the dispatcher to call off the search. By the time he'd finished explaining, he felt utterly drained, although he knew his problems hadn't ended. They wouldn't, until he straightened out everything with his son.

Ten minutes later, Mac carried an exhausted Corey inside.

"You found him," Rob exclaimed in a whisper.

"At the bus station."

"Corey and I are going to have some hot chocolate," Lori announced. "Thanks for coming over, Rob, Gail."

"We were glad to help," he answered.

Mac watched Lori usher Corey toward the kitchen, hardly believing the night had ended so well when it could have turned out far differently.

Rob slapped Mac on the back. "Get some rest," he advised. "If I were you, I'd take tomorrow off."

"I think I will." His absence would put a strain on the rest of the team, but what choice did he have?

Gail hugged him. "Good night, Mac."

"Thanks again," he said, before quietly closing the door behind them. He drew a deep breath and followed the sound of voices. Corey was sitting at the table, eating scrambled eggs and toast and drinking a cup of hot chocolate.

The sight of his son digging into his food as if he were starved made him want to fire Mrs Partridge all over again.

He sat beside Corey, gratefully accepting the mug Lori pushed in front of him. The plea in her eyes reminded him to treat Corey gently when his relief made him want to lash out instead. He nodded once to signal he understood her message and her smile instantly returned.

"I talked to your aunt Liz," Mac began. "She told me that you want to live with her."

"I don't like Mrs Partridge." Corey's lower lip quivered as he brandished his fork. "She threw out my special cake. There were still three pieces left. I hate her and I won't go back!"

"Mrs Partridge is gone," Mac said. "I fired her."

Corey stared at him as he wiped his nose with the back of his hand. "You did?"

Mac nodded. "Yes, I did."

Corey glanced at Lori as if he couldn't believe this news and she smiled. "I was there," she said to reassure him. "She's already moved out."

His eyes closed and he wilted before Mac's eyes. Obviously, his resolve to reach Liz had held him together when nothing else would.

"I know you were unhappy," Mac continued, "and I'm really sorry that you were. It's my fault because I didn't listen to you in the first place, but running away wasn't the answer."

Corey's eyes flew open. "But, Dad, I had to do something. When you didn't come home, I didn't know if you'd ever do anything. I was afraid nothing would change and I just couldn't take it any more."

"I understand. I didn't handle this whole thing very well. I'd expected Mrs Partridge to be another Martha when she wasn't. For that, I'm sorry. I should have delegated more things at the hospital than I did and I'm sorry for that, too. The question is, are you willing to give me another chance or not? I know I don't deserve one, but it's up to you."

Mac's question hung in the air like a wisp of smoke on a calm day. He gripped his mug with both hands and hoped that he wouldn't snap off the handle while he waited for Corey's reply.

"You'll let me choose?" Corey asked, sounding suspicious. "Really and truly?"

Mac didn't want to, but Corey's happiness came first. "Yes."

Lori interrupted. "This sounds like too big a decision to make at two-thirty in the morning. We're all tired and having a hard time thinking clearly. Now that Corey knows about Mrs Partridge and your plans, Mac, why don't we let him sleep on it?"

"All right." Not eager to hear bad news, Mac readily agreed. "Is that OK with you, Corey?"

Corey nodded.

"Then we'll go home—"

"Can we stay here?" Corey asked in a small voice.

"An excellent idea," Lori answered. "It's late and the sooner you get to bed, the better." She smiled at him. "You can have my room."

"Is it OK, Dad?" He glanced at Mac, his expression unsure.

Mac gave him a half-smile. "Sure."

Lori rose. "While you freshen up, I'll find a shirt for you to wear. Mac, maybe you could help Corey find the towels and such?"

Corey probably knew his way around Lori's bathroom better than he did, but Lori obviously understood how difficult it was for him to let Corey out of his sight. Suddenly, Mac couldn't hold back. As soon as Corey slid off his chair, Mac grabbed him.

He closed his eyes as once again he hugged him close and breathed in his little-boy scent. "Hell, Corey, if I'd lost you, I don't know what I'd have done." His voice choked and his eyes burned. "I love you, son."

"I love you, too, Dad," Corey answered.

Slowly, Mac released his hold and held Corey at arm's length. "No matter what happens, don't ever forget it."

Corey touched the corner of his father's eye. "You're crying, Dad." He glanced at Lori. "You are, too," he said in obvious surprise.

"These are happy tears," she said with a sniffle as she brushed the moisture off her cheeks.

Mac nodded. "So are mine."

Lori stepped forward. "Sorry, Mac, but I can't wait. I need a hug, too." She wrapped one arm around Corey and ran her free hand over his hair, his face and his back, as if assessing whether he was in one piece. "You really are OK? Nothing's hurt or scraped or—"

"I'm fine," Corey told her.

She cleared her throat and smiled through her tears. "I'm glad. I don't mind telling you, I've never been so worried in my life. You're not supposed to give me gray hair until you're a teenager."

Corey peered at Lori's tresses through narrowed eyes. "You're fooling me. There's no gray."

"What a relief," she exclaimed. "I was lucky this time."

Corey's smile and giggle sent a fresh surge of relief through Mac. He'd come so close to losing someone else he held dear. The thought was enough to make him want to grab Corey and hug him again.

Lori slowly turned Corey loose. "It's late for you, young man, and I'm missing out on my beauty rest. You two guys can use the bathroom first and then it's time to call it a night."

After helping Corey wash his face and tug on the old T-shirt Lori had supplied, Mac helped his son crawl under Lori's blankets. *Lucky kid,* he thought as he eyed her mattress.

It didn't help matters when she bent over the bed to hug

Corey and he had an excellent view of her curves. "Pleasant dreams, sweet prince," she said softly.

As he kissed Corey's cheek, it occurred to him that this could be a nightly event if they were a family. His plan to convince her to accept his proposal had been derailed, but now, more than ever, he was determined to make it happen.

"Goodnight, son." He followed Lori to the door and left it slightly ajar behind him.

Mac's physical and mental exhaustion hit him hard. It was time to drive home, but as he picked up his coat from the sofa where he'd flung it he discovered that he couldn't slip it on. "I should let you rest, but it seems as if I can't bear to leave him, even though I know he's safe."

"Then don't," she said kindly. "Stay the night. My bed is big enough for the both of you."

He should go. If he slept in his own bed, he wouldn't breathe in Lori's scent or picture her snuggled against him.

On the other hand, the thought of staying in his house all alone held zero appeal. He hesitated. "You don't mind?"

"Not at all. You're too tired to be on the road anyway."

He was, even if there wasn't much traffic this time of night. "I can't thank you enough for everything. I hated to bother you when it was so late, but I just couldn't face this alone."

"I wouldn't have forgiven you if you had," she told him. "He's as important to me as Ronnie is." Without giving him an opportunity to reply, she said, "You mentioned something about delegating more of your work at the hospital. What did you mean?"

"I'll give more responsibility to Josh. The hospital will scream about their budget, but I'll insist on locum coverage until we hire and train at least two more people. Somehow we'll make something work."

"And what about Corey? Are you going to look for another housekeeper?"

"It will depend on whether or not he wants to live with me." He doubted if he'd ever fully trust a housekeeper again. That left begging Martha to return, if only for a few weeks, or swallowing his pride and depending on Lori. He wanted to propose again but, as she'd said earlier, they were too tired and their emotions too close to the surface to make any decisions now.

"He wants you."

Mac shrugged, wanting to believe her but not completely able to do so. "I'm afraid I'm not as confident as you are."

"I know you're giving Corey a choice, but what do *you* want?"

He frowned. "For him to stay with me, of course."

"Then how will you manage?"

He ran his hands through his hair. "Right now, I have no idea. All I know is that I can't go through another night like tonight."

"Neither can I. I'm just so very thankful that it ended well."

"That makes two of us."

"I've been thinking..." she said slowly.

Mac watched her hand flutter to her throat, as if whatever she intended to say was difficult. He waited.

"I've been thinking," she repeated. "Not just these last few hours, but ever since you hired Mrs Partridge. Does your proposal still stand?"

It was as if she'd read his mind. Or he'd read hers. Hope surged, but he tried to hold it to a manageable level.

"Yes, Lori. It does."

Her smile seemed uncertain. "Then I accept."

CHAPTER NINE

Lori had never seen Mac at a complete loss before, but she'd obviously thrown him off his stride. She should have waited until he'd recovered from the stresses of the evening before she hit him with something else to consider, but she could only chalk up her impulsive statement to her own exhaustion. Before she could backpedal with a suggestion to discuss it tomorrow, a small smile of satisfaction softened the weariness on his face.

"Are you serious?" he asked, as if afraid to believe what he'd heard. "What changed your mind?"

Her laugh sounded forced to her own ears. "Of course I'm serious. As for changing my mind, do my reasons matter?"

How could she admit that his love for Corey had made the difference in her mind? If he could love his son—and admit it—then she had hopes of hearing him profess the same thing to her. What better way to ensure that a deep, abiding devotion sprouted than to be responsible for planting the seeds and watering them with a daily measure of her own affection?

Of all the people he knew in town, of all the friends he could have called to help him deal with Corey's disappearance, the fact that he'd sought out *her* implied a special bond between the two of them. He might not proclaim everlasting love, but she was obviously more than a mere friend and companion.

"No, but you can't blame me for being curious. After all, you said you wanted a grand passion."

Lori smiled. She *did* have a grand passion, but sharing that tidbit would probably make him ill at ease and she didn't want their relationship, such as it was, strained in any way. It was best if she didn't answer directly.

"As you said," she began, "a marriage based on mutual respect and friendship isn't a bad thing. And we have the added bonus of a powerful chemistry between us, so at least we'll be able to stand looking at each other over the breakfast table."

"Will that be enough for you?" He sounded cautious, which was understandable. After hearing her go on and on about heart-throbbing passion, he was bound to wonder if she'd be satisfied with anything less.

How kind and considerate for Mac to be concerned about her lost dreams. If she hadn't realized how much she loved him before now, that alone would have convinced her. In any case, if he occasionally had trouble sorting out his priorities, at least he admitted his mistakes and took responsibility for them to the point where he was willing to do the right thing, even at great personal cost.

Even if it meant accepting another woman in his beloved Elsa's role.

He might consider their marriage one of convenience, a mutually beneficial business arrangement, but to her it would be more than that. It would be *real*. When she said her vows...to love and cherish...she would mean them from the bottom of her heart.

His eyebrows drew together as he frowned. "Lori?"

"Oh, sorry," she said, leaving her thoughts for the moment. "I was just thinking. What did you ask?"

"If you would be willing to settle for less than you wanted. Less than you deserve."

"I know what I'm doing," she said, without hesitation. She'd turned him down before because she'd been afraid that she'd look back and regret not holding out for the big prize, but as she'd agonized during those hours when Corey had been missing, she'd thought of how she'd feel if Mac disappeared from her life. It hadn't taken but a moment to realize that she'd suffer far greater regret if she lost the family and husband she could have had. If the situation wasn't completely the way she envisioned it, it was up to her to turn those dreams into reality.

"I hate to sound selfish," he said with a grin, "but I'm thrilled about your decision. And I'm not saying that because I expect you to be a live-in housekeeper."

"That's comforting," she said dryly.

"I'll do my best to be a good father to Ronnie."

She nodded. "I know, but I should warn you. She's taken all the things her friends have told her about their fathers and built this composite image of what that role entails. I'm afraid she has rather high expectations."

"We'll work it out."

Lori hoped so. "If you don't mind, though, I'd rather not tell the children until Corey decides if he wants to live with you or with his aunt."

Mac's dimple appeared in spite of the stubble lining his face. "Are you trying to wiggle out of our engagement already?"

She chuckled. "No, but if Corey insists on living with his aunt, then we should look at the situation in a different light. However, that wasn't why I suggested waiting."

"Oh?"

"I don't want to influence his decision," she said simply. "If he knows we're getting married, or that we're considering it, he'll vote to stay. His feelings for you are the issue here, otherwise you'll always wonder what route he might have chosen if I hadn't been a factor."

"I'm willing to pull out whatever magic rabbit it takes for him to stay with me."

"I'd want to do the same for Ronnie," she admitted, "but you can't manipulate him. One day he'll wake up and figure out what happened, and then what?"

"OK. We'll do it your way." Mac reached out and pulled her close. "How did you get to be so wise?"

"Experience," she said promptly, aware of how her heart rate had doubled.

"Normally, I'd seal a deal with a handshake, but I think I'd rather kiss you," he said.

She couldn't take her gaze off his mouth. "I'd rather you did, too."

His breath seemed to surround her and she closed her eyes as she lifted her chin. Her lips met his and the tender contact sent liquid fire flowing through her veins until it seemed as if every bone in her body had melted. The rough texture of his whiskers against her fingertips as she stroked his face reminded her that this wasn't a dream or a figment of her imagination.

It was magic. Pure magic.

As his hand began exploring, she didn't object and, in fact, wanted to satisfy the ache he'd created inside her. Initially, she'd seen him as a lost soul, as someone who needed her, but she'd only been partially correct.

She needed him as much as he needed her. She needed to feel cherished, and wanted, and desired, and, heaven help her, MacKinley Grant made her feel all of those things.

But was he thinking of her in his arms, or of Elsa?

Slowly, she stiffened and his hand moved from her breast to her side.

"Moving too fast?" he asked.

Not if you know who's in your arms. "I'm afraid so," she apologized, hoping it wouldn't take her long to hold first place in her future husband's thoughts.

"Sorry. Under the circumstances, marriage will be quite an adjustment for both of us."

In her opinion, blending two families was more of a major lifestyle change than a mere adjustment, but she simply nodded.

"My house is larger than yours," he continued, "and unless I give up my den or we move, we'll only have three bedrooms."

It wasn't difficult to guess where he was headed with his remark. "I know."

"Then you understand we'll be sharing a room."

She nodded slowly. "Yes, but I think we should talk about that."

His eyes darkened with a combination of curiosity and suspicion. Instead of answering, he simply raised one eyebrow.

There was no way to say what needed to be said, except to blurt it out. "I know that you don't feel the same for me as you did Corey's mother. And while I'd admit that we share a physical attraction, I don't want to make love until I'm sure you won't mistake me for your first wife."

"With the sparks flying between us, once we're in close quarters..." He raised an eyebrow. "You're not being realistic."

"Maybe not, but those are my terms."

Mac released a drawn-out sigh before he finally nodded. "All right. When can we get married?"

"A month?"

"A month?" he echoed. "Why wait?"

"I refuse to run off to Las Vegas or rush to the judge's chambers at the courthouse." It reminded her too much of her first marriage and that hadn't turned out to be the wedding of a lifetime. "I may never have a church filled with guests and orange blossoms, but I want my daughter to see that one shouldn't enter into marriage lightly or treat it like just another appointment in one's day."

"All right. We'll do it your way. If we can move things forward, though..."

Lori didn't see any way possible to hold the ceremony before the end of November but rather than argue, she agreed. "If we find a minister, and *if* we find a place that's available, and if we can make all the other arrangements like a cake and flowers and dresses then, yes, we'll move the date forward."

"I can live with that." Mac cupped her face and brushed her lips with his, as if sealing their agreement with a kiss. "Since we've settled those issues, I vote for a few hours of sleep."

Lori glanced at the clock. Four a.m. If she skipped her morning toast and coffee, she had two and a half hours until her alarm rang and three hours until she had to report to work.

It was less than ideal, but she'd managed before. If Fridays weren't already short-staffed, she'd have called in sick, but they were, and so she wouldn't. Perhaps they'd have a quiet day—one was long overdue.

Yet, as she lay next to Ronnie and heard her soft breathing, she couldn't sleep. How could she? Mac lay in the next room, most likely wearing next to nothing. If that vision wasn't enough to hold the sandman at bay, the thought of lying next to him in a few short weeks did.

Lori functioned on pure determination during her shift. Her eyes burned from her relatively sleepless night and her muscles ached as if she'd run a marathon, but as she settled into her routine, her discomfort faded. Taking care of her patients, especially Hannah Drescher, she was reminded of how minor her aches and pains and worries really were.

She completed her latest round of observations on Mrs Drescher, who'd undergone a Caesarean section two hours earlier because of a prolapsed umbilical cord. Normally, C-section patients received a spinal or epidural anesthetic but, because time had been critical, she'd received a general anesthetic and had landed in Lori's recovery room.

Sadly, her baby hadn't survived.

Although Lori hadn't seen the infant or been involved with it in any way, the loss affected her because it reminded her of the hours when they'd worried over Corey. Even without the parallels between this woman's experience and her own, caring for patients like Hannah was tough because the mother had gone through so much, only to leave the hospital empty-armed and broken-hearted.

In the meantime, Brad's pager was about to drive her and Talia nuts. It had rung every five minutes for the past twenty.

"Do you suppose he's realized that he left it on our desk?" Talia asked as she shut it off for the third time.

Lori sighed. "Who knows? Knowing how difficult he can be to reach at times, I suspect this little trick is more habit than accident."

"Can't you complain to Dr Grant about him? Seeing as you have his ear, so to speak..." Talia grinned "...he'd listen to your gripes before he'd listen to mine."

"Believe me, I will," Lori said before she stifled her latest yawn.

"Must have been some party you went to last night."

Lori managed a smile. Everyone knew better than to link her and parties in the same sentence, which was why Talia constantly teased her about it. "Mac's son decided to run away from home last night and we went looking for him."

"Omigosh. Did you find him?"

"At the bus station. By the time the excitement had died down and I went to bed, it was four o'clock."

"No wonder Dr Grant called in sick today."

"Yeah. I'm not sure what details he wants to share so, please, don't mention it to a single soul."

Talia pantomimed locking her mouth. "My lips are sealed. Is he OK?"

"He's fine," Lori replied, purposely refraining from sharing her news. She didn't want anyone to know of the upcoming wedding until she'd talked to Ronnie and Corey. Although she hadn't said so to Mac, she hoped he wouldn't say a word until they were all together.

Blythe came in and spent the next few minutes assessing Hannah for discharge to a regular hospital room. Her Aldrete score, which was based on activity level, ability to breathe and vital signs, had been constant for the last thirty minutes, so Lori expected Blythe to sign her release. She did.

"Your husband is waiting for you in your room," Blythe told her kindly.

"And the baby?"

"He's there, too."

Lori knew that the parents would be given time with their son's body to grieve in private. She felt badly for them, imagining how easily she could have been in the same position had they not found Corey. Between his disappearance, the prospect of marrying Mac and a sleepless night, her emotions had gone into a tailspin. It wasn't difficult to sympathize with the distraught mother.

She and Blythe wheeled Hannah to the maternity wing and left her in the care of her husband and the OB nursing staff.

To cheer herself after taking care of Hannah, Lori walked past the nursery. She peeked through the window and saw five babies lined up in their bassinets, all looking like wizened gnomes in their pointed little caps and color-coded pink or blue blankets.

She'd always dreamed of bringing home four precious bundles. Two boys and two girls. While Corey wasn't bundle-sized any more, looking after him would let her fulfill half of her wish.

Idly, she wondered what it would be like to carry Mac's baby. They'd never discussed having more children, which, considering their arrangement, seemed premature. She might sleep with him, but it would be the only activity going on in their bed.

He wasn't particularly pleased by her conditions. In fact, he'd seemed rather disappointed, which was rather flattering. However, as he'd said, marriage would be an adjustment for both of them so, as far as she was concerned, consummating their relationship needed to wait for the right moment.

She quickly forgot the notion of babies when she returned to the PACU and ran into Brad, whose mood was more hostile than grumpy.

"Why didn't you let me know my pager was here?" he demanded.

"How were we supposed to do that?" Lori asked. "We didn't know where you were and we certainly couldn't page you."

"You have heard of using the hospital intercom?"

His sneer grated on Lori's already tired and stressed nerves. His eyes were bloodshot, which was only to be expected. Last night he'd shared call-back with Josh and the surgical team had been busy with an emergency splenectomy and an ectopic pregnancy. She hoped she looked better than he did.

"We tried it once, but you didn't answer," Lori retorted. "For all we knew, you were making out in the broom closet with your pharmacist friend."

"Speaking from personal experience?" he asked snidely.

Lori gritted her teeth. Responding would only fuel the flames of his obvious discontent. "Don't you have someplace you should be?"

He turned and, without answering her, stormed from the unit.

"Geesh!" Talia exclaimed. "I wonder what set him off today?"

"It's hard to say. I'm just glad he's gone." As she fell into the routine of looking after a new patient, she slowly pushed him out of her mind. Fortunately for her, Brad's and Josh's next case went to Talia.

The rest of the day passed quickly as she watched over people who'd undergone appendectomies, hip replacements and a variety of other procedures. All were routine, except for a woman who bled excessively after her hysterectomy.

Lori could have used an extra set of hands as she monitored her closely for shock, dealt with the lab and hung several units of blood and fresh frozen plasma. Finally, the woman's condition stabilized and Lori turned her over to the intensive care nurses at the end of her shift.

Three o'clock hadn't come soon enough for her, but she knew that her evening—her entire weekend—would be too busy to catch up on lost sleep.

She parked in front of the school and watched her daughter race across the school grounds toward her car. Ronnie normally exhibited high energy, but today she seemed more excited than usual.

"Mac said we were going to have a surprise tonight," Ronnie announced breathlessly as she scrambled into the front seat. "What is it?"

Lori hadn't expected Mac to be awake before her daughter had left the house, but he apparently had. "I'm not sure what he was talking about," she prevaricated.

"Will we find out when we get home?" she asked.

"Maybe. If Mac and Corey are still there. Otherwise I'm sure you'll learn what it is this evening."

Ronnie wiggled in her seat belt. "I bet it's a puppy."

Lori smiled at her daughter's speculation. "What makes you think you're getting a pet?"

"'Cause Mac said it was for all of us. What else could it be?"

"Somehow I don't think a dog is your surprise," Lori said. *A brother, or a father, but not a dog.* Then, because she was curious, she asked, "What else did Mac say this morning?"

"Not much. He ate breakfast with me and Susannah. His eggs don't taste as good as yours do. He doesn't melt cheese on 'em."

"Maybe you can tell him to add it next time."

"I s'pose. Are you sure you don't know what the present

is?" Ronnie asked. "If you told me, I'd pretend to be surprised. Honest."

Lori laughed at her daughter's earnest expression. "We'd better wait for Mac, don't you think? He'll probably want to tell Corey, too."

Apparently satisfied by her response, Ronnie speculated on the mystery during the drive home. Her excitement only grew once she saw Mac's black Lexus parked in front of the house. Lori could hardly keep her in her seat until she stopped the car.

Ronnie raced to the porch and through the door before Lori stepped foot on the concrete. By the time she walked in, Ronnie had discarded her coat and school backpack on the floor and was tugging on Mac's hands, begging for him to reveal the surprise. Corey looked on, appearing equally as excited with his smile spread from ear to ear.

"I'll tell you as soon as you put your things away," Mac said. With a hoop and a holler, Corey stuffed Ronnie's coat in the closet while she ran her backpack to her room. Their feet thundered across the floor as they returned to stand near Mac.

"Sit," Mac directed.

The two obeyed instantly, although they both wiggled with anticipation.

"First of all," Mac began, "Corey has an announcement."

The youngster nodded as he looked at Lori. "I've decided to stay with my dad. I got to thinking that if I lived with Aunt Liz, Dad would get lonely. Us guys should stick together."

Lori held out her arms and hugged him as he walked into her embrace. "He'd miss you terribly," she affirmed, "so I'm glad to hear your decision."

"Me, too," Ronnie said. "What a great surprise."

"Oh, but there's more." Mac raised an eyebrow at Lori and she responded with a shrug and a wave for him to proceed. "Lori and I have talked this over and we're getting married."

Ronnie's eyes widened. "Really?" she asked, looking at her mother, then Mac, and back to her mother for final confirmation.

"No kidding?" Corey studied his father, as if trying to determine if this was a joke.

"It's true," Lori said, and as she spoke, Ronnie shared a congratulatory high five with Corey.

"Sweet," the little girl crooned.

"Then you don't mind if we become a family?" Mac asked.

"We were hoping we would," Ronnie admitted.

"How soon are we getting married?" Corey asked. "Will we have to dress up with ties and everything?"

"I'm not sure of a date," Lori admitted. "We haven't started planning yet."

"That's not entirely true," Mac said. "I called several ministers this morning."

"You did?"

"Only to get information," he answered quickly, to Lori's look of surprise. "The soonest date available for a church wedding is next August."

"Next August?" the children wailed. "We have to wait that long?"

"We could always make an appointment with the justice of the peace," Lori offered. "We could host the reception at your house."

"No justice of the peace," he said firmly. "Our ceremony will be different."

He remembered the circumstances of her first wedding and his thoughtfulness touched her. "It's all right, Mac," she said softly. "I wouldn't mind."

"You might not, but I do. Which is why I made another call to the hospital chaplain. His schedule is open for next Saturday and he offered us the use of the chapel."

"Next Saturday?"

"A week from tomorrow," Mac confirmed. "I know it's short notice, but if we don't schedule him, we'll have to wait until after Christmas."

"Can't we have it next week?" Ronnie begged.

"I vote for next week, too," Corey said.

Mac raised one eyebrow as he cast an amused glance at Lori. "The decision is yours."

"I don't know if I can find anything for us to wear by then," she said weakly as she glanced at her daughter.

"You'll look beautiful no matter what you wear."

She wondered if he'd think the same if she walked down the aisle in jeans or, better yet, a uniform.

"Then there's the flowers and the cake. How will we ever be ready?" Her voice rose.

"I'm sure we can find a bakery to handle a cake and a florist to make a bouquet," he soothed. "As I said, though, it's up to you. Surely, if we put our minds to it, the four of us can accomplish a lot this weekend."

"Yeah, Mom. We can," Ronnie assured her. "If two heads are better than one, then four are two times as good."

Lori bit her lower lip as she weighed all aspects, including the pleading looks on the children's faces. "All right," she agreed. "Next Saturday it is."

"Yippee!" The two youngsters danced around the room before they headed down the hall, returning a minute later.

"Can Corey and I have a dog?" Ronnie asked Mac. "We'd take really good care of one."

"I'm sure you would."

"Then it's OK if we get a puppy?"

Lori held her breath, wondering how Mac would handle her daughter's first of what would probably be many requests.

"Your mother and I have to discuss it first."

"She'll say yes if you do," Ronnie said, turning her pleading big brown eyes on him.

"We'll talk about it after the wedding," he promised. "We need time to settle into our new household before we bring a puppy home."

"All right. We'll wait." She nodded. Although she appeared willing to postpone their discussion, she clearly wouldn't forget it.

The two children headed back down the hall and Lori sank onto the sofa. "You handled that well."

"Hey, I wasn't about to walk into that without a conference."

"Good idea." She rubbed the back of her neck and sighed.

"Are you OK?" he asked.

"Yeah. I'm just feeling a little overwhelmed right now. A sleepless night and a rotten day are catching up with me."

He sank beside her and drew her close. "What happened?"

"What didn't?" She explained about the Drescher baby. "Brad was in rare form, too, which didn't help."

"Oh?" He tensed.

"He didn't do anything wrong that I'm aware of," she hastened to say. "He was just being obnoxious. No big deal."

"You don't like him very much, do you?"

"It's not a question of like or dislike. There's something about him that raises my hackles, although I can't put my finger on it."

"If he bothers you again, let me know." Mac grinned. "There are perks associated with marrying the boss."

"And what would those be?" she teased.

"For starters, dinner out. We have a lot to celebrate."

Mac lowered his mouth close to hers. A tingle started down her spine as she anticipated his next move, a move she wholeheartedly wanted. Liquid heat seemed to flow through her and she felt as if they were surrounded by an indescribable form of energy.

Ronnie's voice effectively doused the sizzle and the moment passed, as it undoubtably often would with two children in the house.

Lori attempted to break away, but Mac held her firmly in his embrace as if he were establishing his territory. Ronnie would have to get used to seeing her mother as Mac's wife. "What did you need, Ronnie?" he asked.

"Can we have pink flowers at the wedding?"

"I don't know," Lori said. "We'll have to see what the florist can arrange."

"If Corey carries the rings, what will I get to carry?"

"We'll figure out something," Mac assured her.

"Melanie wore a white dress at her mother's wedding. Can I wear a white dress, too?"

"We'll look for one tomorrow."

"What are you going to wear, Mac?" Ronnie wanted to know.

"A tuxedo, I suppose. Why?"

"Just wondering." She paused as she studied the two of them seated on the sofa. "Should I start a list of what we need to do?"

"Good idea," Mac said. "Be sure and put your dress at the top."

Ronnie's dark eyes flashed with excitement. "OK. I'll get a piece of paper." She hurried down the hall, presumably in search of writing equipment.

"She'll be back in a minute. You do realize how difficult it will be to get all of us to agree on any given subject."

"We'll negotiate. They might as well learn now that in any family there's give and take."

Ronnie and Corey returned and their quiet, intimate moment passed. For the next hour Lori watched the dynamics of their small group, pleased to hear Mac patiently spell each word for her daughter to painstakingly record on her list. He was so different from Glenn, so much more interested in Ronnie as a person. She would thrive under Mac's attention.

As for Lori, perhaps it wouldn't take him long to realize that he had more room in his heart for her than he'd thought.

CHAPTER TEN

"You look really pretty, Mommy," Ronnie said as she stood beside Lori in the chapel's vestibule.

Lori smiled down at her daughter. "You do, too, sweetie."

"It's nice that we match," Ronnie told her. "Right down to our flowers." She sniffed the red roses in her miniature version of Lori's bouquet.

"Yes, it is," Lori agreed. That alone had been a minor miracle. The first bridal shop she'd entered had the cocktail-length ivory satin dress on display and she'd fallen in love with it. So had Ronnie and fortunately the manager had been able to overnight express a child's size dress from another store.

All in all, everything had gone smoothly, in spite of Corey's refusal to wear pink rosebuds in his lapel because "pink was for girls". Mac had convinced Ronnie that pink flowers, pink candles in the chapel and pink cake was too much pink, so she chose one item in her favorite color—one layer of the wedding cake would be strawberry. Lori decided to carry red roses and fill the chapel with white candles and tulle.

Talia gave the baby's breath in Lori's chignon a final pat. "You look gorgeous. Are you ready?"

"Yes, but if I don't have a chance to tell you, thanks for everything. I couldn't have pulled this off without you and Gail."

"We'd never forgiven you if you had," Talia said with a smile before she peeked into the chapel. "Now, I see Mac and Corey at the front, so it's time." She kissed her cheek. "Be happy."

Ronnie headed down the aisle, past the pews filled with family and a few close friends, as the string quartet played a wedding song. Lori fell into step behind her daughter, her gaze drawn to the man who waited at the end of the short walkway.

Mac stood tall and straight, looking quite handsome in his black tux. In a few short minutes he would be her husband.

A husband. Was she doing the right thing or making a mistake? Had she rushed into this arrangement too quickly?

Her first step faltered as she tried to read Mac's inscrutable expression from this distance.

Slowing her pace, she studied his face. This past week, his features had become almost as familiar as her own, and right now she saw what few others probably noticed. His smile seemed forced and a question appeared in his eyes.

Was he having second thoughts as well?

Ronnie stumbled over the floor runner and Mac's attention swung onto her. His smile of encouragement was the same sincere smile she'd seen all week, the same smile when he'd patiently spelled words for Ronnie's list and had settled arguments between tired children. Yes, she was doing the right thing.

She hardly heard the music or saw the guests as she glided toward the trio awaiting her. For a moment she wondered what life would hold for them, but she knew one thing as well as she knew her name would be Lori Ames Grant—the future would be what she made of it and she intended it to be glorious.

She reached the front and placed her hand in Mac's. He threaded her arm through his as he bent his head to speak in her ear. "Is everything OK?"

Seeing his tension and worry, Lori smiled at him. "More than OK. It's perfect."

This time his grin was as bright as the twinkle in his eyes.

The minister cleared his throat. "My dear friends, we're gathered here tonight to celebrate a most joyful occasion…"

"I must say, Mac," Liz told him during a rare moment alone during the wedding reception, "Lori is a treasure."

Mac's attention strayed from his dark-haired sister to his wife of thirty minutes as she mingled among their guests. She'd never appeared more radiant as she greeted each one. Occasionally he'd hear her laughter and feel a tremendous thrill spread throughout him. She was his.

"I agree."

"I realize this was a rushed affair after Corey's escapade," she continued, "but I hope you two got married for the right reasons."

As far as he was concerned, they had. If he didn't feel the same hot passion that he'd done as a youth, then it was no one's business but his own. He was content and as far as he knew, Lori was, too.

"If you're trying to be nosy, Liz, don't bother because I'm not going to discuss my marriage with you or anyone else. The kids are happy, we're both satisfied—let's leave it at that."

"She loves you, you know."

Her comment brought him up short. "What?"

"Lori loves you. I can see it in her eyes."

The subject made him uncomfortable. "Her eyes always sparkle like that."

"Think what you will, but when she sees you, there's a different kind of sparkle."

"You're imagining things."

"Not at all. Does it bother you to know how she feels about you?"

He fought the urge to run his hand through his hair. *Hell, yes, it did.* He hated to think of how marriage to him might have short-changed her. At times he couldn't believe that she'd accepted his proposal, but he wasn't one to question good luck. After all, he'd been honest from the beginning. Her decision had brought them to this point.

He answered nonchalantly. "Why? Should it?"

"You tell me. For the record, the idea of a whirlwind romance might fool everyone else, but not me. I've been pushing you to get married for years and until a few weeks ago you were dead set against it."

"Women aren't the only ones who have the prerogative to change their minds."

"If you don't want to admit the truth to me, I understand, but, whatever your reasons, I'm glad you married her."

"And I'm glad you approve." He grinned.

"Just remember—don't make comparisons. Lori and Elsa are two different people."

Mac groaned. "Give me a break, sis. I don't need a counseling session today."

"I'm just giving you something to think about," she said innocently before she straightened his bow-tie. "Now, don't forget. We'll bring Veronica and Corey to the house on Sunday morning. Are you sure you wouldn't rather have the hotel room instead of us? We'll stay at your place with the kids."

"Lori wants to handle it this way." The rules of a traditional honeymoon didn't apply to their marriage, but he didn't want to broadcast that information. His colleagues—and hers—assumed he had swept Lori off her feet and, whether it was due to male ego or consideration for Lori's pride, he refused to correct their misconception. If they wanted to believe that he intended to make love in every room of his house instead of limiting himself to a hotel suite, they could. No one needed to know they would probably spend their hours unpacking and reorganizing his household.

"Suit yourself. But let me tell you, once the kids are around, your time alone is virtually non-existent."

He'd already noticed.

Liz glanced across the room. "I'd better check on the munchkins since I don't see yours or mine. I promised Lori I'd keep them out of trouble." Before he could reply, she left.

Mac remained in his place where he could watch Lori interact with their guests. She was beautiful, inside and out, and he couldn't deny his attraction to her. While he enjoyed being with her both at home and at work, he was convinced that his physical need for her was just plain lust, fueled by years of celibacy. Love had nothing to do with how easily his body responded to her smile and gentle touch.

He expected Ronnie and Corey to act as buffers in the days and weeks ahead, just as they had for the last seven days. The nights, however, would be the worst. He'd wanted to exchange his queen-sized bed for a king-sized, but his frugal wife had refused. He was certain he'd spend many sleepless hours lying beside her, inhaling her light floral scent and stopping himself from reaching for her.

And, oh, how he wanted to reach for her. He wanted it so badly that at times he ached. He hadn't realized when he'd agreed to her terms that his marriage of convenience had become so utterly *in*convenient. For the sake of his sanity and his water bill, he intended to revisit those conditions before too many weeks passed.

Lori had made the right choice in suggesting they spend their so-called honeymoon at home. For appearances' sake, they wouldn't leave the house, but at least he wouldn't be confined to one small room.

He watched her approach, her eyes shining as brightly as the expression on her face.

She's in love with you.

Liz's comment echoed in his head and his emotions alternated between pride and guilt. Their marriage seemed full of risks and potential difficulties, almost like a heart attack waiting to strike, but it only took the brilliance of

Lori's smile for his concerns to fade until he could hardly remember what they were.

Their marriage might be unorthodox but, one way or another, he intended to make it work.

Lori's steps faltered as she gazed at her husband's suddenly fierce expression. "Is everything all right?" she asked.

"Everything's fine." He glanced at his watch. "It's getting late. Shall we say goodnight to the kids?"

"Good idea," she said calmly, although inside she was a mass of nerves. She didn't know what was harder to deal with—leaving Ronnie in the care of Mac's sister or knowing that in a short time she'd be alone, really *alone*, with Mac for the first time since she'd known him. Her plan to make him see her and not his first wife had seemed so simple when she'd thought of it, but now that the moment was almost at hand, her courage was faltering.

Yet if she wanted the future she'd always dreamed of, she couldn't *not* proceed.

It was eleven o'clock before Lori walked through the door of her new home. "The wedding was lovely," she told Mac as they placed the leftover cake on the kitchen counter. "The cafeteria staff did a wonderful job. When Chaplain Hardy suggested I call them, I had no idea they could pull off something that impressive."

He grinned. "Then you didn't expect a traditional tiered cake, fancy table decorations, the ice sculpture or the punch fountain?"

"Not at all. If St Anne's staff realizes how capable the food service can be, they'll boycott the stuff they usually serve." She reached up and began removing the pins holding her chignon in place.

"Let me," he said.

She stood still, conscious of his nearness as he plucked the baby's breath and bobby pins out of her hair. As it tumbled down her shoulders, he asked, "Better?"

"Much."

"Do you want to use the shower first?"

"OK. I'll need you to unzip me. I can't reach." She presented her back to him, hoping that he wouldn't wonder how she'd managed the task all these years.

His hands lingered on the satiny fabric of her gown and his fingers fumbled with the hook and eye at her neckline. She smiled when he inhaled sharply as he lowered the zipper.

"Thank you," she said again, before she strolled toward the bedroom they would share. He may have agreed to her terms about postponing the physical side of their relationship, but she didn't intend those conditions to hold for ever. If all went according to plan, it wouldn't take him long to realize that the person lying beside him wasn't a memory but a flesh-and-blood woman who loved him.

From the way his eyes drank in her appearance as she sat in bed thirty minutes later, wearing the peignoir she'd purchased on her wedding dress shopping expedition, her initial attempts to gain his attention had succeeded.

"If you'd rather I slept in Corey's room," he said slowly, "I will."

She hadn't thought of that possibility or else she wouldn't have given Corey and Ronnie permission to spend the night with Mac's sister. "It's up to you, of course," she said, crossing her fingers that he wouldn't choose that option, "but we may as well begin as we mean to go on."

"You're right. I just didn't want you to be uncomfortable."

If he only knew. "I can handle it, if you can."

When Mac simply nodded, Lori relaxed. The excitement of the day caught up with her and her eyelids grew heavy as she listened to the water running in the master bathroom. The moment he returned, clad only in a pair of boxer shorts, his dark hair lying in damp disarray against his head, her lethargy vanished.

Her mouth went dry at the sight of her husband's bare chest at the same time an insane desire to run her hands over his pectorals and through the dusting of hair on his skin struck her.

Her scheme had backfired.

It was quite possible that she'd find her plan more difficult to follow than Mac would.

He crawled in beside her and she struggled to keep from rolling toward him as the mattress dipped in his direction.

"Tired?" he asked.

"Not really." Actually, she was wide awake.

"We could watch television."

"Good idea." Maybe a movie would take her mind off the man who lay close enough that she could feel the heat emanating from his body.

He clicked the remote control to the small television set on the dresser facing them. "I don't normally watch TV, so I'm not even sure if this works any more."

It did and he advanced through the channels until he found a classic Second-World-War era comedy featuring Bing Crosby and Danny Kaye. "How's this?"

"It's fine." Lori snuggled under the covers and fought the urge to move in close to Mac as he folded one arm under his head. Gradually, she relaxed, partly due to the humorous program, the comfort of the bed and her own exhaustion. Dimly aware of Mac clicking off the television at the end of the movie, she snuggled deeper in the warm cocoon she'd made for herself.

"Lori?"

The calming thump in her ear shifted tempo. "Hmm?"

"Careful with the knee."

Knee? She roused herself enough to take stock of her surroundings. An instant later, she came fully awake. Mac's heartbeat had been the thump lulling her to sleep, and she was delightfully toasty because she'd draped herself over him.

To add to her horror, her leg rested on his groin and her knee covered a strategic spot. It also was embarrassingly obvious that at least this portion of his anatomy wasn't ready to sleep.

"You're wide awake, aren't you?" she asked.

"Some parts more so than others," he said wryly.

She raised her head to meet his gaze and he immediately kissed her. The temperature between the sheets rose and she opened her mouth to allow him entrance. Before she realized what was happening, she found herself flat on her back with Mac's hand cupping her breast. She thought of protesting, but the protest died unspoken. This was what she wanted.

Suddenly, he stopped. Her sanity returned. Remembering her condition to their marriage, embarrassment filled her at how Mac had shown more restraint than she had.

"I really didn't mean to wind up all over you," she said. "I was cold and you were so warm..."

He captured her chin so that she couldn't avoid his gaze. "You don't have to apologize, Lori Ames Grant. We *are* married."

The significance of Mac using her name didn't escape her. He knew exactly who she was, and who she wasn't. The question was, was she truly convinced?

"Yes, but we both agreed to stay on our sides of the bed. And—"

"And we're not going to be able to ignore this thing between us," he said softly as he stroked her cheek.

It would be easier to ignore a tornado passing down their street. "I agree."

"So what do we do?" He caressed a path down her neck to the valley between her breasts.

"Separate beds?"

His pained expression was almost comical. "That wasn't quite what I had in mind."

"Maybe you should spell it out. So there's no misunderstanding."

His gaze grew intent. "You know what I want. Before you say anything, I'd like to remind you of your own statement. 'We should begin as we mean to go on.' As a warning, though—if we proceed, we can't go back."

Lori had planned to surround Mac with love in the belief that it would return to her. Now she wondered if withholding the best expression of that love would only delay the very thing she hoped to achieve.

"Then I suppose I should follow my own suggestion," she said softly.

His grin was filled with pure male satisfaction as he lowered his mouth to hers.

Lori had never complained about his kisses. They'd always generated enough power to curl her toes and melt her knees. This one, however, was different. It was as if he'd been holding himself back all along.

Dimly, she was glad she was lying down because she simply couldn't have stood under his onslaught. He touched her as gently and carefully as if she were made of hand-blown glass, taking his time to search out every sensitive spot on her body.

His mouth trailed down her neck until he reached the hollow at the base of her throat. Her skin overheated as his fingers deftly untied the peignoir and slid it off her shoulders. The skimpy lace nightgown didn't stand a chance. It disappeared just as fast until minutes later she lay bared to his hungry gaze.

If only she'd been thinking and had asked for him to turn off the bedside lamp. The light wasn't particular strong, but it was bright enough for him to see the imperfections that childbearing and age had left.

"You're beautiful," he murmured. Without waiting for her reply, he continued from where he'd left off.

Lori ran her hands along his long, lean form, reveling in

the feel of his hard muscles under her fingertips. They fit together perfectly, like two pieces of a puzzle.

Each stroke of her hand seemed to generate as much a response in him as his touch created in her. Before long, the gentleness they shared gave way to a fierce eagerness that demanded release.

She was ready. More than ready. "Please, Mac," she moaned. He'd created such a need inside her that she simply couldn't wait any longer. "Now."

At her plea, he didn't hesitate. He slid inside her and the sensations that had been building coalesced into a single, earth-shattering explosion.

Later, after the tremors had subsided and she lay snuggled against him, she completely changed her honeymoon plans. Unpacking and reorganizing had dropped to the bottom of her list.

The next few weeks brought small changes to their routine. Susannah's babysitting arrangement continued although she now looked after two children instead of one. Mac went to the hospital at the same time so he could either take on the early surgical cases or complete his paperwork. He left the later ones for Josh who, being single, preferred coming to work later in the morning. Barring an emergency, Mac would arrive home by late afternoon, or at least early evening.

After dinner and homework, Lori usually organized a family activity to fill the hours until bedtime. While it did her heart good to hear Mac say to Corey and Ronnie "I love you" when he made the rounds with her to tuck them in at night, she still waited to hear those words addressed to her.

Be patient, she told herself. After clinging to a belief that he'd never love again for eight long years, it would take longer than a few weeks to change his thinking. Although she hoped for a miracle, she took it one day at a time.

Her relationship with Mac wasn't the only thing she had to take one day at a time. Brad Westmann, who wasn't Mr Congeniality on the best of days, was still the proverbial thorn in Lori's side. His surly attitude hadn't improved, although poor Talia had borne the brunt of it.

"I heard Brad's probation got extended," Talia announced on Wednesday.

"Yeah, but he is allowed to handle some cases alone," Lori explained. "Mac and Josh still make a point to drop in on him during his procedures. It's going to be a while before they let him take call again."

She grinned. "Speaking as a newlywed, I wish they would. I wouldn't mind if Mac was home a few extra evenings."

"I'll bet. You've made him a new man."

"Don't be silly," Lori said, although she was flattered by the compliment.

"I'm serious. He's more approachable. Why, he asked the other day if I had plans for Thanksgiving. Until then, I didn't know he even realized that we still celebrated the holiday."

Lori laughed. "He has changed a little."

"More than a little. Aren't you glad the school has their 'Donuts for Dads' and 'Muffins for Moms' program?"

"More than you'll ever know."

"Would you mind cutting the small talk and paying attention to what you're here for?" Brad interrupted in a hard tone.

"There's not a lot we can do until a patient arrives," Lori said, although his condescending manner irritated her. He wasn't her superior, so he had no right to issue orders anyway.

"If you have time to gossip, then you have too much time on your hands."

"We weren't gossiping," Talia protested.

"Oh, yeah? Or were you comparing notes on the next complaint you intend to file on me?"

"We weren't discussing you at all."

"Of course not." He sounded sarcastic. "You save that to tell the boss at night."

Lori bristled. "I beg your pardon. We have better things to discuss than hospital staff."

"Yeah, right. As if I'm going to believe you."

Fortunately for Lori, one of the surgical nurses poked her head in the doorway. "Brad? They're ready for you in room one. Dr Morrison is waiting."

He sent Lori a hateful look, then left, pushing the double doors so hard they banged on the walls.

"Whew," Talia said. "He's on the warpath today."

"It must be the stress of staying out of trouble."

"Either that or we're finally seeing the hidden side to his personality. Now, enough about him. What are you wearing to the Firemen's Ball on Saturday?"

"Looks like everyone in town turned out tonight," Rob remarked as he sat next to Mac at their table in the corner of the town's convention center. Gail and Lori had taken advantage of the band's intermission to locate the powder room.

Mac glanced around the huge room. People filled every available space as far as he could see. On the other hand, he hadn't expected it to be otherwise. The Firemen's Ball was more than a social gathering for the community. Proceeds from this annual event allowed the fire department to purchase needed equipment above and beyond their budgeted funds. The CairnsIRIS helmet purchased last year, which allowed the wearer to see thermal images, had been instrumental in saving the lives of two victims who'd been trapped inside a burning house. Most people understood how the incident could have ended tragically for the elderly couple, and many were eager to help the department raise money.

"I'll say."

"Lori looks pretty tonight," Rob commented. "New dress?"

Mac shook his head. "She refused to buy one because she claimed she hadn't worn out the one she already owned." In actuality, Mac had instructed her to use her salary to pay off Glenn's remaining debts. Although she hated the idea of not contributing financially to the household, she'd agreed. Now she refused to spend a single penny on anything she deemed unnecessary, even if it meant waiting for new clothes. In any case, if being able to write "Paid In Full" on each of Glenn's IOUs made her happy, then Mac was satisfied.

"Gorgeous and thrifty." Rob shook his head. "How did you manage that?"

Mac grinned. "Pure luck."

"I guess. I have to admit, though, marriage definitely agrees with you."

"I can't argue. I don't know how she did it, but my house was just a house until she moved in. Now it seems like a home. Lori is absolutely wonderful."

Rob slapped him on the back. "I can tell the honeymoon isn't over yet."

Mac couldn't stop the Cheshire-cat grin that spread across his face. After three weeks, he still couldn't get enough of her. Everything about her—her scent, her soft skin, the way she nestled against him, the breathless sigh she made at the height of their passion—only made him want her more. He would gladly spend the next month with her on a deserted island where nothing and no one could intrude.

"Yup." Rob nodded vigorously. "From the look on your face, you have it bad."

Mac stopped daydreaming. "What are you talking about?"

"Don't you know? You're in love. Unless I miss my guess, you've got a major case of it."

He wanted to deny it, but how did one confess that he didn't love his own wife?

Or did he?

"I'm not sure what I feel for Lori is love," Mac admitted, watching his friend's response.

Rob stared at him as if he'd grown two heads. "You're not sure what you feel is love?" he echoed. "You said for a long time that you'd never love anyone except Elsa, but do you really believe you'd have married Lori if you didn't love her to some degree?"

Rob's question hung in the air, giving Mac food for thought. It had taken a long time for him to realize that he loved his son, but he did. Now he loved Ronnie because she was his daughter by marriage. Each night, as he helped Lori tuck them into bed, telling them that he loved them had become a part of the ritual that he didn't hesitate to perform.

Now he wondered if Lori had been waiting to hear those words every night before they went to sleep. He'd never thought of saying them because he simply couldn't say what he didn't know in his heart was true.

"I loved my first wife," Mac said slowly. "I felt completely different with her than I do with Lori."

"Of course you did. You were young, met a woman who turned you on and, bingo, instant passion meant you were in love. For a lot of us love sneaks up and catches us unawares. Sometimes it comes with a bang and other times it comes on a whisper."

Could it possibly be that simple?

The question was, did he *want* to love her? He'd locked away that emotion to protect himself from heartache, but Lori had shown him how denying his love for his son hadn't lessened it at all. Was this the lesson he was supposed to learn where she was concerned? Had she breached his defenses without him realizing what she'd done?

Don't make comparisons. Lori and Elsa are two different people. Liz's comments at their wedding now surfaced as clearly as if she'd just spoken them in his ear.

It was apparent that he'd been measuring his experience with Lori against his experience with Elsa. In essence, it was almost like weighing the use of benzodiazepines to barbiturates. Both were valuable drugs and vital to patients, but they weren't alike and weren't meant to be.

Yet it seemed disloyal to Elsa's memory to admit that he loved another woman. No wonder Lori had insisted on not consummating their marriage until she knew that he didn't see her as anyone but herself.

With these new doubts, he needed time to sort out his tangled thoughts. He only hoped that when he did he wouldn't destroy something precious.

By Sunday evening, Lori was starting to worry. Mac had been preoccupied ever since they'd returned home from the Firemen's Ball, but he refused to discuss it. She was tempted to call Rob and ask what they'd talked about during their time alone, but she couldn't summon the courage to do it. It seemed like an invasion of Mac's privacy.

She'd hoped that after a day holed up in his office he'd have worked through whatever bothered him, but by ten o'clock he didn't seem in any better spirits.

After crawling into bed beside him, she said softly, "If you want to vent, I don't mind listening."

Mac raised up on one arm. "I know. I haven't been good company today."

"Everyone's entitled to quiet time."

He stroked her face. "You're very special. You know that, don't you?"

Lori smiled. "So I hear."

He kissed her forehead. "If you don't mind, I'm tired."

Lori sensed it was more emotional than physical exhaustion, but she didn't press him. Mac obviously needed to come to terms with whatever bothered him.

"OK. Goodnight. I love you." She recited the same words she always did. He answered the same way he always did—he simply kissed her.

She clicked off her bedside lamp and fell asleep, only to wake several hours later when Mac began tossing and turning. He mumbled something, but she couldn't catch what he'd said so she grabbed his shoulder, intending to wake him.

Suddenly, he spoke a name loud and clear. A name that ripped her heart in two.

Elsa.

CHAPTER ELEVEN

Lori pulled back her hand, unsure of her next move. Should she wake Mac and ask about his dream, or pretend the incident had never happened? Unfortunately, she wasn't good at pretending.

Elsa had been a part of Mac's life, just as Glenn had been a part of hers. It was unreasonable and unrealistic to expect Mac to totally wipe his memories of Elsa from his mind. However, she'd hoped that her love would be enough so that *she* filled his waking and non-waking moments, not his first wife.

Lori couldn't lie beside him, fearing that he'd turn to her with visions of another woman inside his head. This had been her concern when he'd proposed to her and she'd foolishly believed his reassurances on their wedding night because he'd told her what she'd wanted to hear. Now the truth had finally come out—no matter what she did to turn his house into a home, how she mothered his son or how much she loved him—she couldn't break Elsa's hold.

Knowing she'd have to start her day in less than an hour, she slipped off the mattress, grabbed her robe and headed for the sofa. The colorful afghan she'd knitted last winter became her blanket, the armrest her pillow.

Lying there, she thought about her life. For the past month or more she'd been encouraged by Mac's eagerness to spend his rare hours of free time with her rather than hibernating in his den, catching up on paperwork. They'd attended plays, seen movies and gone for the occasional dinner for two. She'd charted real progress by those actions and had believed that it couldn't be long until he realized that what he felt was love.

Obviously, the notion had been wishful thinking on her part.

She shouldn't be angry at him for never saying the words—he'd warned her that it would never happen. Instead of paying heed, she'd ignored that warning. She'd planted hope and watered it with her own love, hoping to duplicate the feelings he'd experienced before, but she'd failed. She should have treated their marriage as he obviously had—an arrangement to benefit their children, with great sex thrown in as a perk. She'd given her heart to him alone, but he obviously didn't want it.

Now what should she do?

Mac turned over and reached for Lori, but her side of the bed was cold. He glanced at the clock, wondering if he'd overslept, but it was fifteen minutes before the time Lori usually rose.

With the remnants of his dream still haunting him, he padded out of the room in search of Lori's comforting reality, only to find her curled up on the sofa.

"Lori?" he asked. "It's six o'clock."

She shot straight up. "Oh. Wow." She finger-combed her hair out of her face. "Good thing you woke me. I don't want to be late."

This was the first time he'd slept apart from her since their marriage, and he didn't like seeing her anywhere but next to him. "Are you sick?"

"No."

"Then what are you doing out here?"

She clutched her robe tightly around her as she stood. "You were having trouble sleeping. I didn't want to disturb you, so I left."

Her explanation didn't make sense. "If I was tossing and turning, you should have woken me instead of leaving yourself."

"It's no big deal. Forget it."

The way Lori avoided his gaze told him that it *was* a big deal and he immediately grew wary. "What's wrong?"

"Why do you ask?"

"Because you're upset."

"It's nothing. You were just talking in your sleep."

"I was?" If he'd repeated part of his conversation with Rob, then he was sunk.

"You only said one thing. A name, actually."

He prayed he'd uttered Lori's name, but she wouldn't have reacted this strongly if he had. "And?"

"You were dreaming of Elsa."

Reality was slowly turning into a nightmare. "Yes, but—"

"I have to get ready or I'll be late." She turned to leave, but Mac grabbed her arm.

"I don't care if you're late," he said tersely. "We need to talk."

"Like we talked after the Firemen's Ball when something bothered you? Or the way we talked yesterday, when you spent the day brooding?"

"I had to deal with some issues."

"Well, now it's my turn." He released her, but he couldn't start the day this way. Without hesitating, he followed her into the bedroom and watched as she walked toward the master bathroom.

"It was a weird dream," he told her. "That's all."

"I'm sure it was, but I can't deal with this right now. I'm sorry." She walked into the bathroom and closed the door.

The set to her jaw cautioned him to give her a few minutes alone. He would have preferred storming the room, but he didn't want to go to work with a black eye from a well-thrown bar of soap.

Mac tugged on his own clothes while he waited impatiently for her to return. As soon as the door opened, he started speaking, although she didn't acknowledge that she was listening.

"Everything was all mixed up. I saw us at our wedding. We were cutting the cake, but just as you held up a piece for me to take a bite, you became Elsa."

She ignored him as she walked to the closet and pulled a scrub suit from the closet.

"In the next scene, she was standing there, taking to Liz. Corey came running up but, instead of going to her, he went to you. And when it was time for us to leave, everyone waved goodbye to her instead of us. I remember feeling sad that she was going, but at the same time I was glad because you were with me." He stared at her. "Bizarre, isn't it?"

She paused, then tugged her tunic top over her head.

"I saw the house where she and I lived when we first got married but, instead of coming home and finding her, I found you. The last thing I remember was that we were both at the hospital and Elsa warned me that you were in trouble." His eyes narrowed "You're not pregnant, are you?"

This time she met his gaze. "No. Under the circumstances, it's for the best."

"Oh. But do you see what I mean about it being odd?"

"Look," she said, "I appreciate that I was worthy enough to share your dream with your former wife. However, all it tells me is that you're confused about who I am and who you want. Unfortunately, life stuck you with me."

"I *chose* you. It has nothing to do with being *stuck*."

She continued as if he hadn't spoken. "One of us can't sleep indefinitely on the sofa, so when I get off work I'm going to buy twin beds."

"I don't understand why you're so upset. You wouldn't be angry if Rob or Gail had been in my dream."

"Because I'm not competing with them."

"You're not competing," he protested. "You have your own place. You're my wife."

"So was Elsa. I may have been the one marrying you in your dream, but Elsa put in an appearance."

"I knew she didn't belong in those scenes. I tried to ask her why she kept popping up, but she'd never answer."

"Fine." She finished tying her shoes and stood. "Tell me how you'd feel if I called out Glenn's name."

"If it wasn't during a moment of passion, then I don't care whose name you call when you're asleep."

"And what happens when I turn to you afterwards? Will you wonder if I'm still thinking of Glenn or of you?"

She had a point. "That wouldn't happen," he said firmly.

"How do you know?"

"Because you love me."

"I appreciate your confidence, but I don't have the same luxury. I don't *know* if you love me."

Did he love her? Rob's comments finally made sense. Elsa had appeared in his dream, but Lori was the one who'd remained with him, the one who shared his house and the one his son knew as his mother. He loved Lori, but his love hadn't come with the same flash of intensity. It had grown slowly but surely, which was why he hadn't recognized it until now.

"I love you," he stated unequivocally. Her unconvinced expression forced him to remember her experience with Glenn. He added, "I'm not saying this because it's what you want to hear."

"Aren't you?" Her tone sounded weary, defeated.

"No."

She turned away, but Mac stopped her before she made it to the doorway. "Let me explain because it's important. I loved Elsa from the beginning, but I suspect now that it was more a combination of lust and her being the first woman who meant something to me. What we had was exciting, I'll admit, but with you it's been an entirely different experience."

"If you're trying to make me feel better, you'll have to work harder," she warned.

"That's why I couldn't acknowledge what was between us," he argued. "At first, I didn't *want* to admit it was love, but Rob pointed out the obvious. You see, my feelings for you grew out of friendship and respect rather than the flames of infatuation. You said that we could look at each other over the breakfast table. Well, I want to do that for the next forty or fifty years, and if that isn't an example of my love, I don't know what is."

Lori's eyes glistened before she stared at a point over his shoulder and rubbed the back of her neck. "I want to believe you."

"Then do," he urged.

She turned her sorrowful eyes toward his. "Right now, though, I can't."

Mac didn't know what else to say, what other argument to put forth. He should have told her over a candlelight dinner, not after he'd called out someone else's name. If the circumstances had been reversed, he'd be leery, too.

The question was, how did he convince her?

"I've got to go."

"I won't let this drop," he warned her. "We'll talk again tonight."

Lori paused, but didn't answer. Mac wanted to wrap his arms around her and kiss her, but he suspected she wasn't ready for such an overture.

It was going to be a very long day.

"You and Mac had a fight," Talia guessed.

Lori managed a smile. "How could you tell?"

"You've barely said more than two words for the last three hours. Plus, when Dr Grant walked in, the air temp dropped twenty degrees."

"You're right. We hit a rocky patch. A *very* rocky patch in our relationship."

"Do you want to talk about it?"

"No." Then she asked, "How can you tell when your husband's being honest?"

"You think Mac lied to you?"

"It's more a case of stretching the truth." She hated to think she'd been as gullible the second time around. Glenn's shoe-box of IOUs represented more than a legacy of debt—it was a shoe-box full of mistrust. What would Mac leave her?

"What did he do?"

"He didn't do anything," Lori said, not willing to mention specifics. "Just answer my question."

Talia shrugged both shoulders. "I suppose it would be the same way you'd know if anyone wasn't being honest. They'd fidget or they wouldn't look you in the eye—unless, of course, they've honed lying through their teeth to a fine art. I've heard con artists can."

Glenn might have fit in the latter category, but Lori was sure of one thing. Mac didn't.

She interrupted before Talia's tangent took them totally off course. "I'm talking about regular people."

"Well," Talia said thoughtfully, "Caleb's voice changes when he's hiding something. Oh, and he always rubs one eye. I figured all this out last Christmas when he was trying to keep me from knowing that he'd bought an engagement ring. The main thing, though, is how you feel in here." She patted the region over her heart.

Lori replayed their conversation. Mac had met her gaze, hadn't fidgeted and his voice hadn't wavered. By Talia's criteria, he'd been honest. Her heart wasn't as sure.

He's not Glenn.

She nearly laughed aloud at her little voice's reminder. All this time she'd been afraid of Mac comparing her to his beloved Elsa, while she'd been guilty of the same crime.

Glenn had always told her what she'd wanted to hear, and although she'd accepted his answers, deep down she'd never been truly satisfied.

Mac wouldn't do the same, her heart told her. It would have been far easier for him to declare undying love when he'd proposed his marriage of convenience, but he hadn't. He'd been honest, brutally so, when a well-placed reassurance would have been the better tactic for a man who was intent on his own agenda.

He could have said that he loved her just as he'd loved Elsa and the issue would have ceased to exist. But no. He'd been forthright and had tried to explain how his love was different, how it was still a love that would last a lifetime.

Mac loved her. He truly loved her.

The realization brought tears to her eyes. "Oh, Talia. He really loves me."

"Well, of course. A blind man could have seen that."

Lori blinked rapidly to clear her tears of joy. "I have to talk to him."

"You'd better hurry. We'll be getting a varicose vein removal and a tonsillectomy before long."

"I will." Lori dashed from the PACU. She wouldn't be able to say much, but she wanted Mac to know that everything was all right.

How could she have faulted him for loving her in a different way? She'd been waiting for the same hot-flash-of-youth sort of love that he'd shared with Elsa, but it hadn't happened. Instead, her love for Mac had crept up on her, too, although she'd recognized it sooner. She had the passion she'd wanted, but it was much like he'd described—the slow, simmering sort that built to a steady, blazing fire.

How could she have missed seeing what had been under her nose?

According to the surgery schedule, his hip replacement case would start soon. Intent on finding him before then, she rushed to the surgical anteroom where the staff administered the pre-op meds. She poked her head through the first curtain, but the area was empty.

Lori went to the next and stopped as soon as she saw Brad. "Have you seen...?" The rest of her question died unspoken as she comprehended his actions.

Brad's sleeve was rolled past his elbow and he was injecting the contents of a syringe into his arm.

"What do you want?" he growled as he turned his back from her to slip the syringe into the biohazard container.

"I was looking for Dr Grant. My gosh, Brad. What are you *doing*?"

He rolled down his sleeve and drew up another syringe full of fluid as if nothing unusual had happened. "I'm getting ready for my patient."

"No, you're not," she protested. "I saw you. What did you take?"

He dropped the filled syringe on the tray and advanced. "You didn't see a thing. Do you hear me?"

Lori shook her head. "I'm not lying for you. You have a problem, Brad. A serious problem."

"I don't either." His harsh tone softened. "This was just something to kill the pain in my back. Some days it's worse than others."

"You can't help yourself to meds whenever you feel like it," she protested.

"Everybody does it. With all the access we have, who's going to know?"

Suddenly, all the inexplicable situations over the past few months coalesced into a picture that she couldn't believe she hadn't seen before. His mood swings, days of inattentive behavior, his willingness to run errands to the pharmacy—they had all been pieces that she hadn't fit together.

"How long has this been going on?"

"Nothing's going on," he insisted.

"Brad," she said firmly, "you have a problem. You

need help. Professional help." She turned to leave, but Brad grabbed her arm.

"You can't tell anyone. It won't happen again."

He sounded sincere, almost pleading, but Lori knew what she'd seen. Even if she believed him—which she didn't—she couldn't remain silent.

"Brad, if something happens to a patient you're—"

"I can handle my job."

Arguing wouldn't get her anywhere. Agreeing with him and gaining his trust might cause him to relax enough so she could break out of his bruising hold. "You're hurting me, Brad."

He grabbed both shoulders and shook her until her head hurt. "You can't tell anyone."

The glazed look in his eyes scared her, as did his superhuman grip. "I won't. I promise."

His expression became more threatening. "You're lying."

"No. No, I'm not."

"You are, too. You've caused me enough trouble. I worked hard for this job and I won't let you take it away." With that, he released her, only to squeeze her throat instead.

Lori tried to pry his fingers loose, but he was too strong and she couldn't get enough oxygen. Her vision turned dark around the edges and she gasped for breath.

"Don't...do...this..."

The pressure around her neck increased and her strength began to waver. *Mac*, she cried inside her head. Before she could form another thought, everything faded to black.

Mac strode into the PACU, intent on finding a chart he'd left there earlier. He also had hopes of finding Lori in a more forgiving frame of mind.

Surprisingly, she wasn't in the unit. He knew her personal code of ethics wouldn't allow her to leave Talia fending for herself with two patients unless it was an emergency.

"Where's Lori?" he asked.

"I don't know. She went looking for you about fifteen minutes ago."

"Did she say what she wanted?"

Talia smiled. "It wasn't work-related, if that's what you're asking."

He wasn't certain if he should be happy or worried that Lori was hunting for him. If she was upset...

"Don't worry," Talia said kindly, as if she'd seen his thoughts reflected on his face. "She has good news."

Mac was relieved. Talia probably knew more than she was telling, but he didn't care. What puzzled him was why, if Lori had been searching for him, she hadn't found him. He hadn't wandered too far from the PACU or the surgery suites all morning. While he didn't believe in premonitions, something bothered him about the situation. The warning from his dream popped into his head.

A monitor beeped and Talia hurried to check it. "When you see her, remind her that I'm a little busy."

"I will."

Following his instincts, Mac decided to take another stroll through his usual haunts. As he approached the pre-op rooms, a muffled crash caught his attention. Immediately, he changed direction and went to investigate. In horror, he saw Lori hanging limply from Brad's hands.

His adrenalin kicked in. "Let go of her," he ordered as he tried to pull Brad's hands away.

"She's not going to tell," Brad threatened, his face red from exertion.

"Oh, my God," a nurse said from behind.

"Call Security," Mac shouted. He had no idea how long Lori had been unconscious, so time was of the essence. Determined to force Brad to release her, he changed his strategy. He threw a punch to Brad's face, and felt grim satisfaction as he broke the man's nose.

Brad howled and clutched his face. Mac caught Lori inches before she hit the floor. In the next instant a crowd of people had gathered, including a security guard, but Mac hardly noticed.

Lori wasn't breathing.

Her neck was red and beginning to show bruises, but she still had a pulse. "Oxygen," he demanded.

"The hose won't reach."

He didn't waste a moment. He covered her mouth with his and gave her several breaths, carefully watching the rise and fall of her chest.

Lori didn't respond.

"Help me get her up," he demanded.

Hands came from all around him and within seconds she was lying on top of a gurney.

Mac fitted the oxygen mask over her face and willed her to breathe. The situation seemed surreal as he waited and watched. This wasn't just any patient he was concerned about. This was Lori. "I want an LMA."

LMA was shorthand for a laryngeal mask airway, which had become the latest in airway crisis techniques. It involved inserting the deflated mask down into the hypopharynx with the index finger as far as possible. Once the operator felt resistance, the cuff was inflated and the tube exiting the mouth secured. Without knowing what, if any, damage had occurred to her trachea, this was a less invasive alternative for establishing adequate air exchange.

Someone wrapped a blood pressure cuff around her arm while he began listening to her heart through his stethoscope. "Hang in there," he told her, hoping she could hear him.

"Here's the LMA." A nurse thrust it at him and he inserted it with an ease borne of practice and training. Immediately her chest began to rise and fall. Mac allowed himself a few seconds of relief, but while they'd overcome the first hurdle, there were more ahead.

"Keep her on oxygen. I want Radiology to take a few pictures, stat."

People scattered to obey. He glanced around to discover Brad missing. "Where is he?" he demanded.

Mac didn't need to mention names. Everyone knew who he was talking about. "Brad's with Security," a nurse admitted.

Satisfied that the man responsible was in custody, Mac focused on Lori. "Come on, sweetheart. Don't leave me now."

Lori was floating in a gray mist. The darkness she'd seen before had lifted, but exhaustion weighed down her limbs and her throat hurt. She wanted to go back to the black void where pain was non-existent, but a voice kept calling to her.

"Lori. You have to hang on."

She didn't want to obey. It sounded far too hard a task when all she wanted to do was sleep.

"Lori. Come back. You can't leave me. I love you."

The deep voice sounded frantic. It was Mac's voice, she realized idly.

"Ronnie and Corey need you."

Mention of the children caught her attention. She really didn't want to leave Ronnie behind.

"*I* need you."

Mac needed her. She liked to be needed. Maybe she should stay for him, too.

"I love you."

She remembered him saying that. Remembered how she'd finally believed him.

"Don't leave me. I couldn't bear it."

No, she couldn't leave, she decided. She couldn't do that

to Mac, not after he'd lost one wife. They had an entire life ahead of them and she didn't want to miss any of it.

She struggled to raise her eyelids but the bright light made it difficult. Finally she opened her eyes and saw Mac's face hovering above hers. He'd never appeared this worried before, not even in an emergency.

He clasped her hand in his and raised it to his lips. "You're back."

She managed a nod. Her voice wouldn't work for some strange reason.

"Don't try to talk. We inserted an airway until we see what's going on."

Again, she gave a single nod.

"Just relax. You're going to be fine." With that reassurance, she drifted away.

The next time she awoke, she was lying on a gurney in the pre-op area and Mac sat in a nearby chair. His hand was warm as he held hers, and as soon as she moved he jumped to his feet and smiled. "Hi."

Her mouth was dry and her throat hurt, but the tubes were gone and her voice worked. "Hi, yourself. What's wrong with me?"

"Your throat is bruised and you have some swelling, but nothing's broken. In a few days you'll be yelling again."

"I doubt it," she whispered.

"I was never so worried in my life," he admitted.

"Me, too." An image of Brad's furious face swam before her eyes and she clamped them tight to shut out the image. In spite of her fear, she had to ask. "Brad?"

"He's in custody. He confessed that you'd caught him taking drugs. Apparently he's been diluting meds and charting doses that he's given himself for quite a while."

No wonder she'd seen a higher incidence of Brad's patients who needed more morphine than others.

"He's on his way to jail and eventually, I presume, to drug rehab."

Raction set in. Her hand shook as she rubbed her eyes. "I was so scared."

Mac gathered her close as if he needed the contact as much as she did. "I know."

"I was so afraid I'd never see you again."

"Me, too."

"Oh, Mac." Unable to hold back her emotions, words failed her and she burst into tears. She hardly noticed how he sat on the edge of the bed and held her.

"Just let it out," he murmured against her hair. "You're safe now. He can't hurt you."

It was several minutes before the fountain inside her slowed to a trickle and she regained her composure.

"Better?" he asked.

"Yeah. Thanks."

He pressed a kiss to the back of her hand. "I love you, Lori."

"I know. I was going to tell you that when I ran into Brad."

"Then you do believe me?"

She spoke fervently as she smiled. "Without a doubt."

"What convinced you?"

"I realized that you're too honest for your own good."

"What?"

"I'll explain later. When I can talk without my throat hurting. Do I have to stay here?"

"Not unless you want to."

"I don't." She wanted her own bed and her husband beside her to keep her living nightmare at bay.

"We'll go home as soon as you're ready to leave."

"What about your surgeries? And Talia?"

"All taken care of," he informed her. "Right now, I want to spend time with my wife, reassuring myself that she's still in one piece."

"A kiss won't hurt me, will it?" she asked. At his answering grin, she added, "Then what are you waiting for?"

She raised her mouth to his, pleased to discover there were times when a doctor would follow a nurse's orders.

One year later

Lori carried the shoe-box of IOUs outside to the patio where Mac, Corey and Ronnie hovered around her ancient barbecue grill.

"You're being awfully slow," Mac teased her.

"Yeah, Mom," Ronnie said. "We've been waiting for *hours*."

"It's only been a few minutes," she replied, dumping the scraps of paper inside the empty grill.

"Yes, dear, but it's cold," Mac told her.

"Weakling," she teased as he pulled the collar of her coat around her ears. "OK. Who's got the matches?"

"We do," Corey and Ronnie shouted together. "Can we light it now?"

"Yes, you may."

The children struck the matches and tossed the flaming sticks into the nest of papers. Fire devoured the notes like a greedy dragon and smoke spiraled into the chilly late afternoon air.

She'd brought these small scraps of paper to her marriage, and now she was sending them and the mistrust they had caused into oblivion, where they belonged. She didn't have room for either in her life any longer.

Mac pulled her against him. "You did it," he said. "I'm proud of you for having the integrity to pay off those debts when no one would have faulted you if you hadn't."

"Thanks. I'm proud of me, too."

As the scraps slowly turned to ash, Mac asked, "What is my frugal wife going to splurge on now that she's debt-free?"

"I'm not splurging on anything," she said. "I'm saving it for a downpayment on a bigger house."

Mac stared at her in surprise. "A bigger house? Isn't this one large enough?"

"It would be, but we need an extra bedroom."

"An extra bedroom? What for?"

Lori threaded her arm through his as she leaned on him. "We're going to have a guest...for about eighteen or nineteen years."

His eyes suddenly gleamed with understanding. "You're pregnant?"

"Dr. Ratna confirmed it this morning. You'll be a father again in about seven months," she said happily.

Ronnie tugged on her sleeve. "We're going to have a brother or a sister?"

"Yes, you are," Lori answered.

The two children whooped and hollered as they danced around the yard, suddenly oblivious to the cold. While they were out of earshot, Lori pressed her hand to the area over Mac's heart. "Do you think you have room for one more in here?"

"With plenty to spare."

As he kissed her, Lori hoped their children would someday discover the joys of a love that came softly and lasted a lifetime.

LIVE THE EMOTION

Modern Romance™
...seduction and passion guaranteed

Tender Romance™
...love affairs that last a lifetime

Medical Romance™
...medical drama on the pulse

Historical Romance™
...rich, vivid and passionate

Sensual Romance™
...sassy, sexy and seductive

Blaze Romance™
...the temperature's rising

27 new titles every month.

Live the emotion

MILLS & BOON

MB3

MILLS & BOON

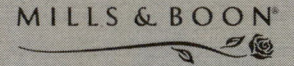

Medical Romance™

THE SURGEON'S SECOND CHANCE
by Meredith Webber

Harry had loved Steph when they were medical students – but she married Martin. Now Steph is a widow – and Harry is back in town…and back in love! Harry knows he and Steph should be together, and he's not going to miss his second chance. He has to prove that she can trust him. But it won't be easy…

SAVING DR COOPER *by Jennifer Taylor*

A&E registrar Dr Heather Cooper isn't looking for love. But when she crosses paths with a daring firefighter she's frightened by the strength of her emotions. Ross Tanner isn't afraid of danger. To him, life is too short not to live it to the full – and he's determined to show Heather that his love for her is too precious to ignore.

EMERGENCY: DECEPTION *by Lucy Clark*

Natasha Forest's first day as A&E registrar at Geelong General Hospital held more than medical trauma. She came face to face with the husband she had thought dead for seven years! A&E director Dr Brenton Worthington was equally stunned. Somebody had lied, and Brenton needs to discover the truth!

On sale 6th June 2003

Available at most branches of WH Smith, Tesco, Martins, Borders, Eason, Sainsbury's and all good paperback bookshops.

MILLS & BOON

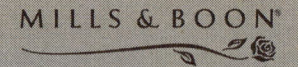

Medical Romance™

THE PREGNANT POLICE SURGEON
by Abigail Gordon

GP and local police surgeon Dr Imogen Rossiter is fiery, beautiful – and pregnant! When she meets fellow GP and police surgeon Dr Blair Nesbitt sparks fly between them…until Imogen tells him she is carrying another man's child. Both are thrown into an emotional turmoil that tests the strength of their love.

THE GPs' WEDDING *by Barbara Hart*

Dr Fabian Drumm and Dr Holly Westwood were happily planning their wedding – until Fabian's mother told him his real father was not the man he called 'Dad' and he had half-siblings in America! Fabian changes his mind about marriage and children – but Holly refuses to give him up!

HER ITALIAN DOCTOR *by Jean Evans*

Dr Beth Bryant is determined to find fault with her new boss – until she recognises him as the drop-dead gorgeous Italian she saw that morning on her way to work! Dr Nick D'Angelo spells sex appeal in the extreme, and his romantic intentions are glaring. But Beth doesn't want to feel the emotions of loving and losing again…

On sale 6th June 2003

Available at most branches of WH Smith, Tesco, Martins, Borders, Eason, Sainsbury's and all good paperback bookshops.

FREE!

2 Books
and a surprise gift!

We would like to take this opportunity to thank you for reading this Mills & Boon® book by offering you the chance to take TWO more specially selected titles from the Medical Romance™ series absolutely FREE! We're also making this offer to introduce you to the benefits of the Reader Service™—

- ★ FREE home delivery
- ★ FREE gifts and competitions
- ★ FREE monthly Newsletter
- ★ Books available before they're in the shops
- ★ Exclusive Reader Service discount

Accepting these FREE books and gift places you under no obligation to buy; you may cancel at any time, even after receiving your free shipment. Simply complete your details below and return the entire page to the address below. *You don't even need a stamp!*

YES! Please send me 2 free Medical Romance books and a surprise gift. I understand that unless you hear from me, I will receive 4 superb new titles every month for just £2.60 each, postage and packing free. I am under no obligation to purchase any books and may cancel my subscription at any time. The free books and gift will be mine to keep in any case.

M3ZEB

Ms/Mrs/Miss/Mr .... Initials ....
BLOCK CAPITALS PLEASE

Surname ....

Address ....

....

.... Postcode ....

Send this whole page to:
UK: The Reader Service, FREEPOST CN81, Croydon, CR9 3WZ
EIRE: The Reader Service, PO Box 4546, Kilcock, County Kildare (stamp required)

Offer not valid to current Reader Service subscribers to this series. We reserve the right to refuse an application and applicants must be aged 18 years or over. Only one application per household. Terms and prices subject to change without notice. Offer expires 29th August 2003. As a result of this application, you may receive offers from Harlequin Mills & Boon and other carefully selected companies. If you would prefer not to share in this opportunity please write to The Data Manager at the address above.

Mills & Boon® is a registered trademark owned by Harlequin Mills & Boon Limited.
Medical Romance™ is being used as a trademark.